League of CHAMPIONS

THE GLORY GARDENS SERIES
(in suggested reading order)

League
of
CHAMPIONS

BOB CATTELL

Illustrations by
David Kearney

RED FOX

A Red Fox Book

Published by Random House Children's Publishers UK
61-63 Uxbridge Road, London W5 5SA

A division of The Random House Group Ltd
London Melbourne Sydney Auckland
Johannesburg and agencies throughout the world

Text copyright © Bob Cattell 1997
Illustrations copyright © David Kearney 1997

Score sheets reproduced with kind permission of David Thomas
© Thomas Scorebooks 1985

First published in Great Britain by Red Fox 1997

17 19 20 18

Set in Sabon by SX Composing, Rayleigh, Essex
Printed and bound in Great Britain by
Clays Ltd, St Ives plc

THE RANDOM HOUSE GROUP Limited Reg. No. 954009

www.randomhousechildrens.co.uk

ISBN 978 0 099 72401 8

Penguin Random House is committed to a sustainable future for
our business, our readers and our planet. This book is made from
Forest Stewardship Council® certified paper.

Contents

Contents

Chapter One

Until Jo showed up at nets that morning we all thought the season was over for Glory Gardens.

It had been our best year ever. We'd won the North and East County League and then beaten the "Rest of the World" in the "World Cup" – that's what Frankie called our international knock-out competition – earlier this month. We beat Griffiths Hall School from Barbados in a nail-biting final. And we'd lost only one game all season – a fluke win by Mack's Australian team in the World Cup.

But all that seemed history now. Azzie, Marty and I are still playing for the County Under 13s Colts; Clive would be too but he's had a row with Liam Katz, the captain of the Colts, and he's been dropped for the next game. Clive's still sulking and it was no surprise to us that he hadn't turned up for nets – he's never been very keen on practising. Clive's one of the most talented batsmen in the team: like Azzie he's a real natural. But there are times when he has what Kiddo calls 'a bit of an attitude problem'.

No-one was taking practice too seriously that Saturday morning. Frankie was out of control as usual; Tylan bowled more full tosses than he'd bowled all year and all the batsmen were just trying to knock the leather off the ball. Kiddo was disgusted with us. Kiddo's our coach – he's one of the best too – we would never have had so much success without him. But it's hard to forget that he also teaches us French at school and when he gets impatient the teacher in him really comes out.

"Oh for heaven's sake, Frankie Allen," he shouted. "Take that stupid towel off your head and go and have a cold shower."

Frankie grinned wickedly; he was keeping wicket in a sort of home-made turban. "It's this tropical heat," he protested. "I'm protecting my brain."

It was at that moment that Jo arrived.

But before I tell you about it, I'd better introduce the team properly. That's us in the picture.

Back row: *Marty, Tylan, Cal, Jacky, Erica, Mack*
Front row: *Jo, Matthew, Hooker (capt), Azzie, Clive*
In front: *Frankie, Ohbert.*

I'm in the middle, the one holding the League Cup. My name's Hooker Knight and I'm captain of Glory Gardens C.C. and the team's leading all-rounder. The rest of our bowling attack is standing in the back row; Marty Lear's our fastest bowler and

8

Cal's the slowest – he bowls off-breaks. Clive and Azzie, on my left, are the side's star batsmen. In front of them is Frankie, our wicket-keeper and unofficial team clown and next to him is Ohbert. Ohbert is . . . well, you'll find out soon enough.

Jo – she's sitting just behind Frankie on the left of the row – is our scorer, team secretary, fixtures organiser . . . in other words she does everything except play. And, although you'd never guess it, she's also Frankie's sister.

Jo walked over to where Kiddo was standing and glared at her brother. "Francis, get that thing off your head immediately." Frankie looked round sheepishly and unwrapped the towel. He usually obeys when Jo's in one of her serious moods.

She turned to Kiddo. "I've just received this, Mr Johnstone," she said handing him a letter. While Kiddo read it Jo started to explain the 'Champions League' to us. It was the first we'd heard about it.

"It's a knock-out competition for all the county champions in the country," she said. "Because we won the league, we qualify to play in it."

"The final's at Edgbaston on the test match ground," said Kiddo growing increasingly interested. He read the letter again and then looked up at Jo. "And it seems to me you've already entered Glory Gardens for the competition."

Jo went red. "Yes. There wasn't much time so I wrote off immediately."

"So you've got a game here on Wednesday," said Kiddo.

"Yes," said Jo uncertainly. "I . . . I hope that's all right."

"Hurray. Who are we playing?" said Frankie swinging his towel over his head and catching Ohbert round the ear. Ohbert's Walkman went flying and wrapped itself round his neck.

"Saracens," said Kiddo.

"Who are they?"

"They won the South and West County League," explained Jo. "So it's the county play-off. If we beat them we're into the last 16 of the competition."

"But we can't play on Wednesday," said Azzie.

"Why not?"

"We've got a Colts game."

I'd just remembered it, too. We had a big game against Middlesex Colts on the County Ground. Marty, Azzie and I would be playing.

"They'll have to postpone the game," said Marty.

"Don't be silly," said Jo. "It's all organised. If we don't play on Wednesday we forfeit the game and Saracens will go through."

"Never mind, Mart," said Cal with a smile. "We'll just have to manage without the stars for once." Cal's my best friend. He lives next door to us; he's always the first person I turn to if I have any problems with Glory Gardens – which is quite often. We all think Cal ought to be playing for the Colts, too. He opens our batting with Matthew and he was our top wicket-taker in the league. And he knows more about cricket than any of us.

"Who's going to be captain, then?" asked Jacky.

"If you all insist, I'll do it," said Frankie.

Jo stared at her brother coldly.

"On second thoughts, I nominate Cal," said Frankie. No-one argued with that and Cal said shyly that he'd be pleased to be reserve captain.

"But how are you going to put out a team with only nine players?" Marty, as usual, was quick to spot all the problems.

"And that's including Ohbert," said Frankie.

"Don't worry, Mart," said Mack. "I've got plenty of reserves to call on."

"We don't want any of your Aussie friends playing for Glory Gardens," said Marty.

"Oh sorry, does it say something in the rules about no overseas players?" asked Mack sarcastically.

"Not as far as I can see," said Kiddo with a smile. "Who have you got in mind?"

Mack is Australian through and through – but his family has been living here for some time and he's played for Glory Gardens since the middle of last season. He's a good cricketer and easily the best fielder in the side. He reminds me a bit of Jonty Rhodes,

10

especially when he picks up and throws in the covers; as often as not he hits the stumps direct.

"I think Kipper Hawkes might be interested," said Marty. "And Kris Johansen, too."

Both of them had played against us in the World Cup. Kris is a good, quickish bowler; she'd given all our batsmen plenty to think about. And Kipper's a fair left-arm spinner although he doesn't look like one – he's twice as fat as Frankie, if that's possible.

"Great," said Frankie. "You three go off and enjoy yourselves and we'll do the business, won't we, Ohbert?"

Ohbert didn't hear Frankie because his Walkman was turned up to full volume but he saw us all looking at him and gave a big toothy grin.

"We'll need some snacks to keep Kipper going through the game," said Frankie. "Three dozen hamburgers to start with. . ."

"No chance," said Cal. "We all know who'd eat them. You're slow enough behind the stumps already."

By now everyone had forgotten about Nets. Kiddo started telling us everything he knew about Saracens; it wasn't much but as usual it took him a long while to say it. Half way through his speech Gatting began to snore loudly. Gatting's Kiddo's dog. He's rather old and fat these days and he smells a bit strange but everyone's very fond of him – he's Glory Gardens' team mascot. Frankie, standing beside Gatting, started snoring in time with him and it was difficult to keep a straight face as Kiddo droned on. Then Frankie snatched Ohbert's Walkman, put it on and broke into a little dance pursued by Ohbert. At last Kiddo stopped talking.

"I think some of the Saracens players were in Dad's team when we played them," said Azzie. Mr Nazar had picked a strong team for the World Cup and we'd only just beaten them.

As everyone got excited about the competition I began to feel more and more disappointed that I wouldn't be playing. I almost felt like dropping out of the Colts game and playing for Glory Gardens instead, but I knew I couldn't. I was quite pleased that

11

Clive had been dropped by the Colts. Glory Gardens needed all the batting we could find on Wednesday.

———— • ————

Walking home with Cal after Nets I couldn't get the Champions League out of my mind. "I wonder why we didn't get more notice of it?" I said, thinking aloud.

"Jo says she only got the entry form last week," said Cal.

"Why didn't she tell us then? We might have been able to rearrange the Colts game."

"You know Jo. She keeps things to herself until she's certain about them," said Cal. He grabbed me round the shoulder. "Don't worry, we won't let you down. You'll see."

Chapter Two

Ohbert is Glory Gardens' secret weapon but no-one is quite
sure whether he's for us or against us. He has played for
Glory Gardens right from the start and no-one can deny that
he's part of the team but one of the great mysteries is why he
bothers to play cricket at all.

Ohbert is completely hopeless at nearly everything, especially
cricket. If ever a person was born without a single atom of ball
sense it's Ohbert. He's so bad that he'd probably get in the
Guiness Book of Records as the worst No. 11 of all time.

But that's only half the story. Because, on top of that, Ohbert
is unfathomable – that's Cal's word for him. I think it means that
no-one knows what he's going to do next and we certainly don't
– but then neither does the opposition. So when Ohbert's
fielding he'll let the simplest ball run between his legs, but he'll
also sometimes take the most unbelievable catch you've ever seen
just by sticking out his hand with his eyes closed. His batting is
just as peculiar; no bowler can set a plan for him. I've seen him
play a forward defensive to a bouncer and get four leg-byes as the
ball flew off the top of his head. Jo says he ought to wear a
helmet but I don't think much damage can be done to Ohbert's
brain that hasn't already happened.

Between games of cricket and sometimes during them, Ohbert
listens to his Walkman. He and his headset are almost
inseparable – Frankie thinks he sleeps and showers with it on.
With all the weird sounds which are injected straight into his
ears, Ohbert doesn't have much communication with the world

13

as we know it. So we weren't totally surprised when he turned up with his dad to watch the Colts game at the County ground.

"Ohbert," said Azzie spotting him first. "Shouldn't you be somewhere else?"

"Oh but . . . where?" said Ohbert, pulling his Walkman out of one ear so that he could half listen.

"You're playing for Glory Gardens, you idiot," said Marty.

"No, but I can't be. I'm here," said Ohbert.

"Precisely," said Azzie.

Eventually I managed to explain to Ohbert's father, which is almost as difficult as talking to Ohbert, that he had to get Ohbert and his kit to the Priory ground fast because the match against Saracens was starting in half an hour.

Ohbert wasn't my only problem that afternoon. Liam Katz was sick and I'd arrived at the ground to discover I was captain. That meant we had to win. Liam Katz is a brilliant bat and not a bad captain but he thinks the Colts side revolves around him.

Azzie plays the sweep shot to a well-pitched-up ball just outside leg stump. His left pad is thrust down the line of the ball so that it covers the stumps if he misses. When you play the shot try and hit down at the ball in a sweeping motion without aiming too hard – the sweep shot is all about timing and placement.

If we lost he'd never stop telling everyone it was because he wasn't playing. It didn't help to know that Middlesex are one of the strongest Under 13 teams in the country – unbeaten all season.

"Who's going to open the batting in Katzy's place?" said Azzie.

"Do you fancy having a go?" I asked. Azzie leapt at the chance and, after I'd won the toss and opted to bat, he and Olly Sheringham walked out to open the Colts innings.

Try though I did to concentrate on the game my mind kept drifting off to the Priory. Who would Cal bowl first? Probably Jacky and Kris Johansen. Mack had managed to get both Kris and Kipper Hawkes to play for us. That meant we had plenty of bowling but the batting was seriously weak. Cal told me he was going to open with Matthew and himself as usual but that meant Mack would be batting at No. 3 and Frankie at 6.

This was the batting order he'd shown me:

1	Matthew Rose	7	Kipper Hawkes
2	Cal Sebastien	8	Tylan Vellacott
3	Mack McCurdy	9	Jacky Gunn
4	Clive da Costa	10	Kris Johansen
5	Erica Davies	11	Ohbert Bennett
6	Frankie Allen		

A lot was going to depend on how well Erica and Clive batted. I couldn't wait to discover how they got on.

Meanwhile we had Middlesex to beat. Olly and Azzie saw off their quickies and the Middlesex captain brought on his two spinners. Instantly Azzie went on the attack. He's so light on his feet and quick to pick up the flight of the ball that, on his day, Azzie will massacre even the best spin attacks.

At the end of the first hour we had 67 on the board; Azzie had scored 40 of them. He'd been dropped on 28, a difficult low chance at cover point, but otherwise he hadn't put a foot wrong.

Two of his four boundaries came from perfectly timed sweep

shots that gave their fielder at long-leg no chance at all.

With the score on 75 Olly Sheringham was caught behind. That only seemed to spur Azzie on to further heights. He reached his 50 with a lofted pull over mid-wicket and then, when the quickies came back, he hit three perfect drives for four off successive deliveries.

By the time he finally went on 88 – given out lbw trying to hit a slower ball down the leg side – we were completely on top.

"145 for three," said Marty to me as he clapped Azzie in. "When are you going to declare?"

It was a time game, not limited overs, so the normal thing was to declare at tea which was at 5 o'clock but if we could knock another 50 runs in the next half-hour I could declare early and have a few overs at them before the break. I told Youz Mohamed who was next in to push the score along. Our fourth wicket fell on 170 and I joined Youz for the final dash. Four overs later Youz holed out with exactly 200 on the board and I declared. I'd got 17 which included an edge over the keeper and a drive back over the bowler's head which fell only inches short of a six.

By tea we had them on the back foot at 13 for two. Marty clean bowled the opener for a duck in the first over and then they made a complete mess of an easy single and finished up with both batsmen at the same end arguing about which of them had been run out.

"I didn't expect to be enjoying tea quite this much," said Marty. "I hope Cal's doing the same."

"It's a pity Azzie couldn't play both games," I said.

"Perhaps he could rush over to the Priory and bat instead of Ohbert," suggested Marty.

After tea Middlesex went on the defensive. It was soon obvious that they'd decided to block everything and kill the game. A bit negative, I thought, to go for the draw so early. I brought on the spinners and offered them lots of gaps to play their shots but still they played defensively. So I crowded the bat as much as I could. I was at forward short-leg and the umpires kept telling me to get back because the rules say you mustn't field closer than 11 yards from the bat in front of the wicket.

At last Youz Mohamed got the breakthrough with an lbw and a caught and bowled in the same over. Three more wickets fell and Middlesex had slumped to 46 for seven at the beginning of the last twenty overs.

Youz and Marty bowled brilliantly in tandem for the next ten overs without taking a wicket. There were lots of oohs and aahs and appeals for lbw and for bat-pad catches, but no wickets.

"Bowl as slow as you can and give it loads of air," I told Youz. It nearly worked but silly mid-on spilled a relatively easy chance. In desperation I came on at Marty's end and I gave Olly Sheringham a bowl at the other. With five overs to go, at last we got the eighth wicket – a smart stumping by our wicket-keeper, Sam Keeping. Then I bowled the Middlesex No. 10 with a yorker and back came Marty to finish off the last pair. In the end, the luck ran their way; the edges didn't go to hand; the straight balls bounced over the stumps; the lbw appeals weren't given and they finished on 63 for nine.

I wasn't very pleased when I went up to shake hands with the Middlesex captain. I didn't think much of the way they'd played the game, although I didn't say anything. But worse than that I knew we should have won and I kept wondering whether Liam Katz would have done better.

Marty was fed up, too. He didn't think he'd bowled well at the end and, surprise, surprise, he went into one of his gloomy moods.

"Cheer up you two," said Azzie. "Anyone would think we'd lost."

"Might as well have," said Marty. "It was all my fault we didn't win."

Azzie laughed. "Come on, at least we didn't lose. Let's go and see if Glory Gardens can cheer you up."

Chapter Three

Azzie's dad dropped us off at the Priory ground. There was no sign of the players, the visitors' coach – anything, in fact. There didn't appear to be a soul about.

"It must have finished early," said Azzie. But the pavilion door was open; it was strange that no-one had locked up. And then I heard a noise from the home team changing room.

I knew the result of the game as soon as I opened the door. They were all sitting there with blank faces. Cal had his head in his hands. Not a word was spoken; no-one even looked at us. The only sound was the relentless buzz of Ohbert's Walkman.

At last Frankie spoke. "I suppose *you* won," he said quietly, still not looking up.

"No we drew," said Azzie. "What's happened?"

"Well," said Jacky.

"It's like this," said Mack.

"Typical," said Marty. "I knew you'd lose without us. I told you we should have postponed it. I bet you got completely thrashed."

"Well," said Jacky.

"The fact is," said Cal.

"Amazing though it may seem to you," said Tylan.

"WE WON!" yelled Frankie and he leapt up and threw his batting gloves at Marty with a huge roar of triumph. The changing room was transformed; suddenly the three of us were standing with our mouths open in disbelief while the Glory Gardens players laughed and jumped about and all tried to tell

18

us about the game at once.

"If you could just see your faces," said Cal when things had calmed down a bit.

"I thought you said they wouldn't fall for it, Cal," said Frankie.

"I was wrong." Cal lobbed the Glory Gardens score-book across the changing room to me. "Take a look at that, skipper."

"I knew you could do it," said Azzie standing on tiptoes and trying to look at the scores over my shoulder.

"If only everyone had the same confidence in us," said Jacky sarcastically, with a glare at Marty.

I looked carefully at all the details of the score-book. "But you absolutely hammered them," I said, amazed.

"You wouldn't have said that when we were 18 for three. Or when they'd got 50 on the board for no wicket," said Cal.

"Thanks to Ohbert and Frankie dropping two sitters," said Kipper.

"You dropped one, too. And it was off your own bowling," said Frankie.

Jo took over the story. After losing the three early wickets, Glory Gardens had recovered with a brilliant partnership between Clive and Erica. Clive's 59 came off just 42 balls – even Brian Lara doesn't score that fast. Then Erica held the batting together with a bit of help from Jacky and Frankie – although Jo said Frankie had got out to a horrible slog as usual.

"But what about my six?" said Frankie. "It was the biggest one I've ever hit. And it only just missed Kiddo's car. I thought it was going through the windscreen."

"Pity you got out next ball," said Jacky.

Jo gave them both a stare for interrupting her and continued, "Erica got her fifty in the last over of the innings and Kris put on an unbeaten 19 with her for the tenth wicket."

"It's a shame Ohbert didn't bat," said Azzie. "Did he get here in time?"

"Just about," said Jacky. "He was only half an hour late. And he was stunning in the field as usual. He dropped a complete

19

as about the game a little.

"If you could just see your back," said Cal when things had
calmed down a bit.

HOME TEAM	GLORY GARDENS V SARACENS	AWAY TEAM	AT EASTGATE PRIORY DATE AUGUST. 24TH

INNINGS OF GLORY GARDENS	TOSS WON BY G.G.	WEATHER SUNNY

BATSMAN	RUNS SCORED	HOW OUT	BOWLER	SCORE
1 M. ROSE	1·2	CT MORRIS	WARDLE	3
2 C. SEBASTIEN		bowled	L. SIDI	0
3 T. McCURDY		lbw	L. SIDI	0
4 C. DA COSTA	1·2·1·1·4·1·4·4·5·2·2·4·4·(32)2· 1·4·2·1·4·6·(52)3·4	CT CALDERA	BHARATKUMAR	59
5 E. DAVIES	1·2·1·1·1·1·2·2·2·1·2·4·1·(22) 2·1·1·3·2·4·2·1·2·1·4·2·2·1·4	NOT	OUT	54
6 F. ALLEN	4·2·6	bowled	CHEETHAM	12
7 J. HAWKES	1·2·1	RUN	OUT	4
8 T. VELLACOTT	3	bowled	L. SIDI	3
9 J. GUNN	4·4·1·2	bowled	WARDLE	11
10 K. JOHANSEN	1·1·1·1·1	NOT	OUT	5
11 P. BENNETT				

FALL OF WICKETS

	1	2	3	4	5	6	7	8	9	10
SCORE	0	4	18	77	93	102	110	129		
BAT NO	2	3	1	4	6	7	8	9		

BYES	1·1·1·L	4	TOTAL EXTRAS	19
L BYES	4·1·1·1·1·1	9	TOTAL	170
WIDES	1·1	2	FOR	
NO BALLS	1·1·1·1	4	WKTS	8

SCORE AT A GLANCE

BOWLER	BOWLING ANALYSIS · NO BALL + WIDE													OVS	MDS	RUNS	WKT
	1	2	3	4	5	6	7	8	9	10	11	12	13				
1 P. WARDLE	M	·:2	2·· ·:	·W· ·1	X	·2· :·	4· ·1	M	·2·2W					8	2	15	2
2 L. SIDI	W·: W·11	1· ··	4· ··	·⦿· 3··	·15	X	·⦿·+ 4··	·+· ·1·	·4					8	0	30	3
3 K. BHARATKUMAR	·:4 ·1	2·2 ·4·	·12 ··	1· ··	4W·· ·4·	·2· ··	··2 ··	M						8	1	31	1
4 P. NURSE	··1 ·4	4·· 2·	4· 6·3	X										3	0	24	0
5 J. CHEETHAM	··1 ·2·	6W· ·1	··1 22·	··3 ·1	X	1·· 111	1·· ·4·	4· 2··						8	0	35	1
6 K. CALDERA	··2 ···	3·· 1·2	··· ·1	··· 1·1	·⦿· 2W14									5	0	22	0
7																	
8																	
9																	

after an outstretched up there, the ball backwards over his head for four.

"But the true masterpiece was when he ripped up 'The'...

HOME TEAM	GLORY GARDENS V SARACENS		AWAY TEAM	AT EASTGATE PRIORY DATE AUGUST 24TH

INNINGS OF SARACENS **TOSS WON BY** GG **WEATHER** SUNNY

BATSMAN	RUNS SCORED	HOW OUT	BOWLER	SCORE
1 P. NURSE	3.2.1.1.4.1.3.2.1.3.1.2.2	bowled	DAVIES	26
2 A. MORRIS	1.2.1.1.1.1.1.4.2.1.1.2.2.1	RUN	OUT	21
3 D. LOVEGROVE		RUN	OUT	0
4 L. SIDI	6.2	CT GUNN	VELLACOTT	8
5 H. ADAMS		RUN	OUT	0
6 R. BIGGS	4	CT JOHANSEN	VELLACOTT	4
7 F. SKUSE	2.2	CT ALLEN	HAWKES	4
8 K. BHARATKUMAR	1.2.3	NOT	OUT	6
9 J. CHEETHAM	1.4.2	bowled	VELLACOTT	7
10 K. CALDERA		lbw	HAWKES	0
11 P. WARDLE		bowled	McCURDY	0

FALL OF WICKETS											BYES	2.2.1.2.2		9	TOTAL EXTRAS	17
SCORE	1 50	2 50	3 55	4 63	5 63	6 69	7 80	8 87	9 90	10 93	L.BYES	1.1.1		3	TOTAL	93
BAT NO	2	3	1	4	5	6	7	9	10	11	WIDES	1.1.1.1		4	FOR	
											NO BALLS	1		1	WKTS	10

SCORE AT A GLANCE

BOWLER	BOWLING ANALYSIS · NO BALL · WIDE													OVS	MDS	RUNS	WKT
	1	2	3	4	5	6	7	8	9	10	11	12	13				
1 J. GUNN	..3 .1	..2 .1	.+. 1.1	M										4	1	10	0
2 K. JOHANSEN	.2. 1..	.11 1..	.4. ..1	.1. 1.3										4	0	14	0
3 E. DAVIES	..2 ...	... .2.	.2. .2	M	W.W	M								6	3	8	1
4 C. SEBASTIEN	4.. 1..	.1. .1.	.3. .1.	... .22										4	0	16	0
5 T. VELLACOTT	.62 W..	.4. .W1	.2. ...	..4 .2W										4	0	21	3
6 J. HAWKES	..2 ...	.+.2 W.1	.3. .W.											3	0	9	2
7 T. McCURDY	0++ W													0.1	0	3	1
8																	
9																	

sitter at mid-on, then he threw the ball backwards over his head for four."

"But the true masterpiece was when he tripped up Tylan," said Mack. "They were both chasing after the same ball and Ohbert timed his ankle tap perfectly. Tylan did three somersaults. The batsmen couldn't believe what was going on and they both finished up running to the same end."

"And I picked up the ball and ran one of them out," said Clive.

It was only then that Ohbert seemed to notice that something was going on and his eyes, which had been swimming around in their sockets, suddenly focussed on me. "Oh but . . . Hooker, did you know we won?" he said.

"Yes, Ohbert, well done."

Ohbert grinned broadly.

There had been two other run outs – both by Mack who, Jo said, had fielded brilliantly as ever. "That first run out was the big breakthrough," said Cal. "They'd got 50 off 14 overs and we weren't even looking like taking a wicket."

"And after that they went mad and lost ten wickets for 43," said Erica.

"It was suicide," said Mack. "All of a sudden they started batting like Frankie."

"Without his skill and natural technique," said Frankie demonstrating his magnificent six – a big heave over cow corner naturally.

"Isn't that the same shot you played to the one that bowled you?" said Cal.

"Oh yeah? And what was our captain's contribution to the victory? No runs and no wickets, wasn't it?" retorted Frankie.

"Apart from that he hardly put a foot wrong," said Jacky.

"Who do we play next, Jo?" asked Azzie.

"I'll know on Saturday," she said.

Then we told the others about the Colts game and Azzie's brilliant knock. And before long we were making plans for the next game in the Champions League.

You wouldn't have recognised Saturday's net practice from the

22

week before. Now everyone was keyed up and really competitive. Marty and Jacky bowled flat out and all the batters looked in top nick, especially Azzie, Erica and Clive. For once Clive had put in a guest appearance at Nets. He seemed to have cheered up a lot after his fifty although he said Liam Katz would have to grovel on his knees if he wanted him to play for the Colts again.

Kris Johansen was there, too. Kipper Hawkes said he would come but Mack told me not to count on it because Kipper never gets up before mid-afternoon in the holidays.

Jo was the only other person missing. She was doing the "knicker rota" this week – working on Tylan's dad's market stall which, as you've probably guessed, sells mostly underwear. We all do it in turns on Saturday mornings so that Tylan can come to Nets instead of working for his old man every weekend – and we make loads of money for the club. Ohbert's the star of the knicker stall – he's brilliant at getting tips from customers. Selling knickers is the one thing he is really good at and, not surprisingly, he's Mr Vellacott's favourite. Ohbert must have a different pair of underpants for every day of the year by now.

I asked Frankie if Jo knew who we were playing in the next round of the competition.

"Yes, she told me at breakfast."

"Who is it then?"

"Um . . . I think it was an away game against some team, er . . . somewhere," said Frankie.

"Oh good, I'll tell the others," I said.

"Sorry," said Frankie. "I've got so used to ignoring my sister that I suppose I must have just . . . not listened." I resigned myself to waiting until Jo arrived to hear the news.

Kiddo got the lower order batsmen together for some batting practice. "Too many of you are throwing your wickets away with cross-bat swings," he said. "Look at Tylan and Jacky in the last game and that unspeakable shot of Frankie's."

"Are you trying to tell me to bat like Matthew?" asked Frankie. He played a very deliberate forward defensive stroke with his nose nearly touching the ground.

"Not at all. But you need to learn to hit the ball cleanly."

"If I'd connected with that one it would have gone clean over the pavilion," insisted Frankie.

"But it should have gone straight over Woodcock Lane," said Kiddo.

Frankie looked at him. "What do you mean?"

"Look, if you're going for a big hit try and hit through the line of the ball. You might be out caught on the boundary if you don't place it properly but you shouldn't be clean bowled."

He showed Tylan and Frankie how a straight backlift and follow through would reduce their chances of getting out and bring them a lot more runs.

The important thing about the back lift is that it should be comfortable. Most good batsmen pick up their bat in the direction of first or second slip but then it comes down straight in a line with the stumps. If you don't lift the bat high enough there will be no power in your shots but beware of lifting it too high – a good bowler will soon spot that and trap you with a yorker.

This is the follow-through for a lofted drive played straight down the ground. Don't lift your head until you have made contact with the ball and keep your eyes on it until the last moment. Notice how the face of the bat remains open throughout the shot.

It seemed to work. Frankie immediately lifted an over-pitched ball from Jacky straight back over his head and into the trees.

"Take that!" he said punching the air. Next ball he did the same to Cal.

"Don't bowl that old rubbish at me," he chortled. Frankie was thrilled with his new shot. He's got such a good eye he ought to score a lot more runs than he does but he always lets himself get carried away. I wasn't too convinced that he'd remember Kiddo's advice for long in a proper game.

Jo arrived and at last we found out who we were up against next in the Champions League. "It's next Wednesday and we're playing away. I've looked it up on the map; it's about 60 miles."

Our opponents were a team called Old Bodilians; they were the Nottinghamshire Under-13 champions. It was another 40-overs game like the one against Saracens.

"I'll book the school bus for the day," said Kiddo who seemed as excited about the news as anyone.

Jo had a lot more to tell us. "The finals day at Edgbaston is a week next Saturday," she said. "There'll be eight teams left by then. First they'll play in two leagues of four teams. Then the winners of each league play off in the final."

"And then we'll be the champions of England," said Frankie.

"We haven't even qualified yet," said Jo scornfully.

"Perhaps we'd better pick the team for next Wednesday then," I said.

Our selection committee is Jo, the club secretary; Marty, who is vice-captain; and me. It didn't take long to pick a team. We made Ohbert twelfth man for this game although we told him he would be picked for the next one, if we got through. And, as all the regulars were available, Kris Johansen stood down, too. She said she'd come along and watch and she'd like to play for us any time if we were short.

So the batting line-up for the Old Bodilians game was:

Matthew Rose
Cal Sebastien
Azzie Nazar
Clive da Costa
Erica Davies
Hooker Knight
Mack McCurdy
Frankie Allen
Tylan Vellacott
Jacky Gunn
Marty Lear
Ohbert Bennett (12th man)

Chapter Four

The bus left the school gates at 11.30 on Wednesday morning. Kiddo told us all to be there at 11 o'clock, but he might have known that someone was bound to be late. This time it was Clive and Mack who strolled in at twenty past. It was a bit depressing seeing school again before the end of the holidays but once we were on our way we soon forgot about it.

Clive's aunt had made packed lunches for all of us – cardboard boxes stuffed full of things like spicy chicken, slices of pizza and her world-famous chocolate brownies. Frankie scoffed down the lot before the bus had even got out of town.

"I bet you a chocolate brownie that we win," he spluttered through his last mouthful.

"You haven't got any brownies left to bet with, fatman," said Cal.

"And if you eat any more, Francis, you'll split your cricket trousers again. You know Mum said you could mend them yourself next time," said Jo.

Frankie pulled a face at her behind her back and looked sadly at his empty lunch box.

"Does anyone know anything about Old Thingies?" asked Jacky.

"Who?"

"You know, the opposition."

"Old Bodilians," said Jo.

"It sounds like a nursing home," said Azzie.

"They're champions of Nottinghamshire, so they must be

good," said Jo.

"And they won't be going to Edgbaston," said Frankie. "It's tough luck but someone has to lose."

I only wished I had Frankie's confidence. We had a strong team on paper but Glory Gardens had a knack of making a mess of things. Playing for the Colts had made me realise there are a lot of good cricketers around. There's a big difference between playing good local teams like Wanderers and Crusaders and turning out against the best in the country. I wondered, if I won the toss, whether I should bat first. Perhaps I'd wait until I got a good look at the pitch before I decided.

The journey seemed to take forever and it wasn't improved by Frankie deciding to treat us to his non-stop, one-man show. He began with a medley of his favourite songs. Frankie's singing is very loud and all on one note, except when it's the right note and then he sings another one just for a change. He makes the words up as he goes along, too.

After a time Kiddo told him to put a sock in it and so he switched to jokes and magic tricks. The tricks didn't work apart from one where he made Tylan's 50p disappear – although I don't think Frankie knew where it had gone. The jokes were so bad I've forgotten them all apart from this one:

"Doctor, I feel like a cricket bat."
"How's that?"

And that was the best one.

At the ground the entire Old Bodilian team lined up outside our bus like a welcoming committee. They were all dressed in their cricket whites with red and purple striped jackets on top. Frankie said it reminded him of going to Pontins for his holidays and he shouted "Hi-di-hi," out of the window.

After we'd changed, I walked out to look at the pitch with their captain, a big, dogged-looking boy called Jeff Jessy. The first thing I noticed was a large tree about twenty yards in from the boundary opposite the pavilion. "What happens if you hit

28

that?" I asked.

"Four runs." Jeff didn't waste a lot of words. When I asked him what the pitch was like he shrugged and growled, "Low and slow."

He produced a coin and passed it to me silently. I tossed and he called correctly. He thought for a moment and barked, "We'll bat." I followed him back to the pavilion and signalled to Frankie to get padded up.

Jeff was dead right about the pitch. Marty ran in flat out and gave it everything he'd got, but he couldn't get a flicker of life out of it. Anything short just sat up and begged to be hit and Jeff Jessy, who'd opened the innings, took full advantage. At last Marty pitched one up and he was rewarded with his first wicket from an attempted off drive by the other opener. The ball stopped a bit and flew off the top half of the bat in the air straight to Tylan at mid-off.

Jacky got the hang of the pitch more quickly than Marty. He kept the batsmen on the front foot and bowled straight and a good yard slower than his normal pace. None of the Old Bodilians could get him away.

Marty continued to steam in. He takes it personally if he can't get a ball to bounce shoulder high and he kept digging it in short. Jeff hooked and cut without looking in any danger and, after Marty had bowled four overs and taken one for 19, I replaced him with Cal.

Cal often gets a lot of wickets coming on after Marty; it's probably something to do with the contrast in speed and style. Cal bowls very slowly with lots of loop; his bowling may look easy but time and again he tempts batsmen into making silly mistakes. In his first over he had a good shout for lbw turned down and then Frankie missed a stumping. It wasn't an easy chance because he had to take the ball down the leg side. But in the next over he dropped a sitter off Jacky's bowling and everyone groaned. Jacky stood, hands on hips, and glared angrily at Frankie.

"I told you you shouldn't eat before a big game, fatman," said

Cal. "It makes you even dozier than usual."

"It's your bowling," complained Frankie. "It puts me to sleep."

For the first time one or two heads went down. Tylan let one go through his legs and Matthew made no attempt to run in for a half chance at mid-wicket. Luckily Cal and Jacky responded brilliantly. For six overs they tested and teased the batters with good length bowling, pitching it up and offering them the drive.

The score-board crept up to 37, thanks mainly to Frankie letting through a couple of byes and a hopeless piece of misfielding by Jacky at deep square-leg.

But it was a misfield that brought us our next wicket. Their skipper drove Jacky's full toss to the left of Clive in the covers. He moved swiftly to intercept it but trod on the ball and fell over with a cry of pain. The batsman called a single and set off. Clive hurled himself at the ball which had only rolled a couple of paces and threw from the ground. The non-striker hesitated for just a split second but it was enough. The throw wasn't dead over the stumps, but Frankie was too fast for him. He flicked off the bails and his appeal echoed round the ground.

"That was probably too quick for you," said Frankie to Cal. "Wait till you see the action replay."

But Cal wasn't listening. He'd rushed over to help Clive who was struggling to his feet and seemed to be in a lot of pain.

"It's my ankle," said Clive, collapsing to the ground again as his leg gave way. "I think I've sprained it."

Old Sid Burns, our umpire, came and took a look at Clive's ankle and gave it a rub. Clive screamed.

"Shouldn't you keep it still in case it's broken?" said Erica to Sid.

I couldn't make up my mind whether Clive was badly hurt or faking it. He usually makes more fuss than most people. But he obviously found it painful to walk and finally he decided to go off and have his ankle strapped up. Cal and Marty helped him to hobble back to the pavilion.

"Tell Ohbert he's wanted," I said to Cal. A couple of overs

later Ohbert joined us on the field to replace Clive.

"Here comes super-sub," said Frankie at the sad sight of Ohbert zigzagging onto the pitch.

"Super sub-normal," said Tylan.

The new batsman was a complete slogger. He swung and missed several times at both Cal and Jacky but finally he connected with one and it soared over mid-wicket for four. Ohbert chased it all the way to the boundary and then carried on chasing as if his life depended on it. His frantic throw from the side of the pavilion just rolled back over the boundary rope.

At the end of Jacky's spell I decided to try and maintain the pressure by bringing on Erica. She's always accurate and never gives anything away. She got the wicket of the slogger in her first over. He played all round a straight one and lost his middle stump.

Cal continued to whirl away like a windmill from the other end. He was getting quite a bit of bounce, even on this slow pitch. Cal is always thinking when he bowls and he's not afraid to take a risk or two to get a wicket. The new batsman was using his feet to hit the ball on the full so Cal kept pitching it up, giving it more and more air. Then when he saw the striker coming down the pitch again he dropped one flat and short down the off side. It was an easy stumping chance but Frankie dropped the ball. Cal gave Frankie a cold stare but he didn't say anything. He just turned, walked back and ran in again.

We were nearly half way through our 40 overs by the time Old Bodilians's fifty came up and I could see that both batsmen were getting really tense about the slow scoring rate. Jeff Jessy began to take a few chances against Cal's bowling and you could see Cal was relishing the battle. He likes nothing more than playing on a batsman's ego. In his final over the Old Bodilian skipper hit him through the covers for two. The next ball was on the same spot but a little slower and Jeff hoisted it over mid-off for four.

"Do you want mid-off back a bit?" I asked but as I spoke I noticed that mid-off was Ohbert so it wouldn't make much difference either way.

Cal didn't even look at me. He was concentrating hard. "No,

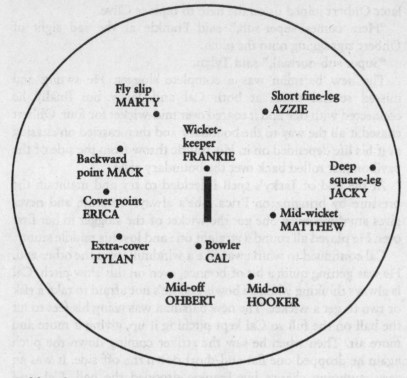

Fly slip
MARTY

Short fine-leg
AZZIE

Wicket-
keeper
FRANKIE

Backward
point MACK

Deep
square-leg
JACKY

Cover point
ERICA

Mid-wicket
MATTHEW

Extra-cover
TYLAN

Bowler
CAL

Mid-off
OHBERT

Mid-on
HOOKER

Cal bowling to a ring of off-side fielders

leave him where he is."

Again he lured the batsman on to the front foot to drive. This time the ball was slower, flighted. Jeff wasn't quite there. The ball went past the outside edge and just tickled the off-stump. The bail dropped, almost in slow motion.

"Out," shouted Cal, jumping in the air and then grinning at me with enormous pleasure. It was a big wicket. Jeff had scored 33 out of his side's 67 and with four down we were calling the shots.

As Cal ended his spell the big question on my mind was, could I risk Tylan? Tylan's got an unbelievable strike rate but he can also go for a hatful of runs. He's an attacking leg-break bowler but sometimes the wheel falls off and he bowls a load of

Cal's high action is the secret to his flight and variation. The movement is like a cartwheel. First the high front arm picks out the target, then the right arm comes over as straight as possible. Some bowlers even brush their ear with their arm as it comes through.

rubbish. I took a deep breath and threw him the ball. His first delivery was wild and wide down the leg side. Frankie couldn't get a glove on it and the batsmen ran two. The next was short and hooked away for three. I saw Jacky and Marty staring at me and I crossed my fingers.

Tylan ran in and bowled again. The ball dipped into the right-handed batsman as he lunged forward and then spun and bounced viciously away from him. There was the faintest of nicks and Frankie half appealed as the ball hit his gloves, stopped as it bounced out and then appealed even louder as he caught it on the rebound.

"Talk about luck," said Cal to Tylan.

"What do you mean? It was an outrageous ball."

"I mean it's the first one Frankie's caught all afternoon."

"I'm just beginning to get my eye in," said Frankie.

"It's a pity their innings is nearly over," sighed Cal.

The score crept up through the seventies and eighties but Erica and Tylan weren't giving much away and the overs were running out. In a desperate attempt to push the scoring along both batsmen started to take risky singles. Finally they went for a run that wasn't just risky – it was plain suicide. The ball went straight to Mack and he sent in a low return which knocked out the middle stump.

Three balls later there was an even more amazing piece of cricket. Ohbert was fielding at mid-on to Erica's bowling and the ball was driven hard to his left. For once Ohbert ran in the right direction but instead of trying to stop the ball with his hands he aimed a kick at it on the run. He not only made contact but the ball cannoned straight into the stumps at the bowler's end. The non-striker who was backing up for the run was left stranded. He wasn't too pleased and he looked even more furious when everyone fell about laughing – but then he didn't know about Ohbert. The hero himself seemed unaware of what he had done and he rubbed his toes through his tennis shoe.

With eight overs to go they were 89 for seven. Erica finished her spell with the amazing figures of 8 overs, 2 maidens, 10 runs, 1 wicket. I decided it was my turn to have a bowl, but just like Marty I struggled to find the right length on this slow track and my first over went for eight runs including a four for hitting the tree. Ohbert was fielding out on the boundary this time and he chased after the ball and clattered straight into the tree as well.

"Timber," yelled Tylan.

For a moment it looked as if Ohbert was seriously injured. He lay still on the ground and Gatting, who had been sitting under the tree, wobbled over and gave him a lick. But then, just as everyone was about to rush to his assistance, Ohbert got up and walked away waggling his head from side to side and grinning as if nothing had happened.

Tylan took another wicket with a smart caught and bowled and then, at last, I managed to get the yorker on the right spot and scattered the stumps.

They finished on 121 for nine. I was pleased to have kept them to three an over, which was pretty good even on a slow track. Everyone had bowled fairly tightly but Erica and Jacky had been outstanding and the three run outs had made all the difference.

"Good performance," said Cal to me. "But if we'd taken our chances we could have had them out for less than a hundred."

At this point the scoresheet shows the top text fragments partially visible.

[When took another wicket with a super catch, and I bowled him at last. I managed to get the yorker on the slow top]

[I finished on 121 for five. I was pleased to have taken two for three an over, which was pretty good even on a slow track.]

HOME TEAM	OLD BODILIANS	V	GLORY GARDENS	AWAY TEAM	AT OLD BODILIANS DATE AUGUST 31st

INNINGS OF OLD BODILIANS	TOSS WON BY O.B.	WEATHER CLOUDY

BATSMAN	RUNS SCORED	HOW OUT	BOWLER	SCORE
1 B. MOLO	2·1·1·2	CT VELLACOTT	LEAR	6
2 J. JESSY	1·1·2·4·2·2·1·2·1·1·2·1·1·1·1·2 2(27)·2·4	bowled	SEBASTIEN	33
3 M. BLACKETT-ORD	1·1·1·1	RUN	OUT	5
4 S. DIPPER	1·4·2·1	bowled	DAVIES	8
5 S. LESLIE	1·3·1·2	CT ALLEN	VELLACOTT	7
6 B. FRIDAY	3·1·1·1	RUN	OUT	6
7 A. TAYLOR	1·1·1·2·2·1·1	RUN	OUT	9
8 N. HAMILTON	1·2·1	bowled	KNIGHT	4
9 R. DE FRIEND	1·2·1·2·2·4·2·2	C & b	VELLACOTT	16
10 M. BOOMER	1·1·1·2·L	NOT	OUT	6
11 J. BAGGINS	1·1·1	NOT	OUT	3

FALL OF WICKETS										BYES	1·1·2·1·1·1·1·			TOTAL EXTRAS	18
SCORE	1 9	2 37	3 47	4 67	5 72	6 88	7 88	8 111	9 113	10	L BYES	1·1·2·1·1			TOTAL	121
BAT NO	1	3	4	2	5	7	6	9	8		WIDES	2			FOR	2
											NO BALLS	1			WKTS	9

SCORE AT A GLANCE

BOWLER	BOWLING ANALYSIS · NO BALL + WIDE													OVS	MDS	RUNS	WKT
	1	2	3	4	5	6	7	8	9	10	11	12	13				
1 M. LEAR	··2 0··1	·2· W·1	·2· 4·	·1· 221	X									4	0	19	1
2 J. GUNN	·1 ··	·· 1··	··2 1··	·· 1··	M	·4·	X							8	1	13	0
3 C. SEBASTIEN	··1 ·2	2··	M	·1 2·3	·1· 2·2	2WW ···	X							8	1	24	1
4 E. DAVIES	··N ·1	··1 2·	M	··1 M	··1 ·1	··1	X							8	2	10	1
5 T. VELLACOTT	43N ···	·1· ··2	·2 ·1	·1 ···	·2 ··2	·1W ··1	·· 1·1							8	0	23	2
6 H. KNIGHT	·2· 24··	··2 ··2	··1 W·1	··· 2·1										4	0	17	1
7																	
8																	
9																	

36

Chapter Five

We found Clive lying on a bench in the changing room. He had a polythene bag full of ice wrapped round his ankle and the moment he saw us he began to moan and wince with pain.

Frankie went over and had a closer look. "Hey, look everyone! It's not even swollen." Ignoring Clive's protests he held up the offending ankle for all to see. "Well maybe it's a bit puffy here," he said prodding the side of Clive's leg. Clive took a swing at him and Frankie ducked and let his foot drop to the ground. "Ouch! You fat idiot, I'll . . ."

"Keep your strength for batting," said Frankie.

I asked Clive if he thought he could bat and he hobbled about a bit and said rather dramatically that he'd do his best but he'd probably need a runner.

"I'll do it," said Frankie. Clive didn't look pleased.

"He said a *runner*. When did we last see you run?" said Cal.

I decided to drop Clive down the order to No. 6. With a bit of luck, if the others batted sensibly, we wouldn't need him.

Kiddo came into the pavilion to give us his pep talk. He told us to remember it was a slow pitch and to cut out the drive unless the ball was right up on the full. "Watch out for the odd one that keeps low," he said. "Especially if you're playing back." He said a lot more, too, but I wasn't really listening. Kiddo's a good coach but he definitely talks too much. I suppose teachers just get in the habit and then they can't stop themselves.

Cal and Matthew must have listened too carefully to Kiddo's

advice. There wasn't an aggressive shot in the first half hour and Matt took five overs to get off the mark. He's always been the most solid and defensive batsman in the team and sometimes his careful approach is just what we need. Clive and Frankie always give him stick for it but Matthew hardly seems to notice. He's very quiet and shy off the field but when he's batting there's no-one more determined. Some days he can be a bit too defensive though, and this was one of them.

After ten overs we had precisely 12 on the board and, with Matthew getting most of the strike, there was plenty for Frankie, Clive and the others to moan about.

"It's worse than going to the dentist," sighed Frankie.

"Definitely more painful," said Tylan.

"Run him out, Cal," shouted Clive jumping to his feet angrily as Matthew turned down yet another quick single. Then he remembered his ankle and limped and groaned a bit in case anyone was watching.

"Cal's getting frustrated," said Mack.

"Who wouldn't?" sighed Tylan.

Mack was right. The slow scoring was putting pressure on Cal and his patience was running thin. He had a couple of wild air shots and then whacked a short one on the leg side for three. But finally he played a horrible heave, head in the air, at a straight delivery and he was clean bowled. He'd scored 14; Matthew was still on 2.

"Play your normal game," I said to Azzie as he went in to bat. Azzie smiled. "Don't I always?"

"The trouble is, so does Matthew," said Frankie.

For two overs Matthew continued to dominate the strike but, at last, Azzie started to get the innings moving. He played a beautifully timed forcing shot off his legs for two and then drove imperiously to the cover boundary. But it was the drive that did for him. The ball must have stopped on him slightly and he hit it hard and low but straight to extra-cover. The fielder took a good, sharp catch diving to his left.

Erica went for a duck. She got a beauty which left her off the

38

pitch and just tickled the edge of her bat on its way through to the keeper. I was in next.

"We're not taking enough quick singles," I said to Matthew. He nodded. What I wanted to say was – get on with it, mate, we need 90 runs at over four an over thanks to you. But I knew that wasn't the way to motivate Matthew. I had to take the initiative myself, just as Azzie had tried to do.

I got off the mark with a leg glance and, by the time I'd played a couple of square cuts smack off the middle of the bat, I was feeling pretty confident. The score-board was starting to move again – we were now on 38 for three off 19 overs. Of course Matthew was still continuing to progress with little nudges and pushes on the off side – his contribution to the score was just seven runs.

Then I got a short one which was probably just going down the leg side and I hooked hard. From the moment I made contact I knew it was six. I felt that sweet throb from the middle of the bat and the ball flew high over the backward square-leg boundary. I don't think I'd ever hit a cricket ball so far. There were whoops of delight from the pavilion and even the wicket-keeper said, "Good shot."

In the next over I got another short-pitched ball and I went for the hook again. This time I got a bit cramped up and the ball took a top edge. I didn't see the fielder on the boundary take the catch because I was running to the bowler's end but I heard the cheers of his team-mates and I knew I was out. I just kept on running towards the pavilion.

The score was looking a bit healthier at 48 for four but I knew we still had a lot to do and seeing Clive hobbling in with Cal as his runner didn't fill me with confidence.

"Leave it to us, Hooker," said Cal. "Long John Silver and I will sort them out."

"Just watch the run outs," I shouted back over my shoulder.

No-one in the team, not even Cal or Azzie or I, can hit the ball as hard and as cleanly as Clive. He's a brilliant player off the back foot and, in spite of his bad ankle, he immediately launched himself at the Old Bodilian bowlers with a series of vicious hooks, pulls and back-foot drives. After 12 balls he'd already overtaken Matthew's score.

But I was right to be worried about the running. Cal and Matthew hadn't exactly built up an understanding between them and Clive was nearly out when Cal forgot to run for a single. After several more close calls the end when it came was almost predictable. Matthew was facing the last ball of yet another maiden over. He pushed it towards extra-cover and Clive called for the single from square-leg where he was standing. Of course it wasn't his call but Matthew's, yet that didn't stop Cal storming down the wicket.

"No," screamed Matthew.

"Yes," shouted Cal even louder. Matthew set off but he was far too late. The throw came in to the bowler and he was run out by nearly half the pitch.

From the reaction on the Glory Gardens' bench you'd have thought one of the Old Bodies' players had been run out – not one of ours.

"Got him!" Frankie celebrated with a little dance. "I knew Cal and Clive between them would see him off."

Matthew returned to sarcastic applause and a few jeers; he had scored just 9 out of our total of 61. I had to agree it hadn't been his greatest innings but I felt a bit sorry for him. I knew that sooner or later we'd need him again to shore up our batting. There are plenty of natural, attacking batsmen in the side but it helps to have a grafter or two to give us balance.

Clive continued to carve up the bowling. He was playing off the back foot whenever he could, pulling and cutting fiercely, but his best four came off a full toss. Clive doesn't miss many of those Clive and Mack had put on 30 runs when Clive called for a quick single – it was the end of the over and he probably wanted to keep the strike. Mack immediately sent Cal back. He was right, too, there was never a single in it. Cal turned and just got his bat in before a direct throw hit the stumps.

The ball bounced away and Clive saw the chance of an

*Everyone will tell you that you have to score off the bad balls —
and a full toss is certainly a bad ball. But don't lose your head
and try and hit it too hard. The secret is to place the ball between
the fielders. Clive picks the full toss off his legs and clips it along
the ground between square-leg and mid-wicket for four.*

overthrow. "Run," he shouted to Mack. Mack charged down the
wicket and then noticed that Cal was still facing the wrong way.
He stopped. Now Cal turned and started to run.

"Stop," screamed Clive. They both did, in the middle of the
pitch and Clive could only stand and watch as the ball was
lobbed to the keeper who casually took off the bails. The
batsmen hadn't crossed so the umpire decided it was Cal – or
rather Clive – who was out.

I told Cal that it was the last time I'd ever choose him as a
runner.

"Why? I really enjoyed it."

"Because I'm exhausted from watching you."

"Well, neither of those run outs were my fault," said Cal.

"Or mine," said Clive.

"Then it must have been a voice from the sky I heard calling for a run," said Tylan.

"Next time I'll be the runner," I said.

Frankie and Mack saw the 100 up and for a time they batted sensibly – even Frankie. It looked as if they would see us home

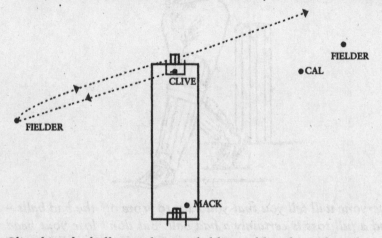

Clive hits the ball straight to a fielder and his throw hits the stumps and rebounds.

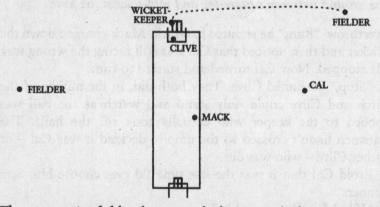

The cover-point fielder throws to the keeper and Clive is run out.

but then, with only 12 needed for victory, Frankie's patience snapped. He suddenly charged down the pitch like a wild rhino, gave a huge heave and tried to lift the ball over the long-on boundary. He missed completely and with his bat raised high he turned to watch the keeper take off the bails.

He could have stumped Frankie ten times before he got his bat back in the crease.

To make things worse, Tylan was bowled first ball off the final delivery of the over. Still 12 to win and now only two wickets left.

Mack faced the whole of the next over and took four runs off it, but he couldn't get a single from the last ball to keep the strike.

"Jacky's on a hat trick," said Jo. "I bet they bring the field in to put pressure on him."

Sure enough the bowler, who had dispatched Frankie and Tylan with the last two balls of his previous over, ran in to a field of two slips, a gully and a short backward square-leg. Jacky got a quick, short-pitched ball just outside the off-stump and he flashed hard at it. The ball could have gone anywhere but it flew off a lucky top edge over the slips for two. He missed the next one and then a leg-bye gave Mack the strike again. The bowler bowled a no-ball and the score ticked on to 118 – four to win.

The next delivery was very short. Mack stepped back and pulled it hard. It flew over square-leg, bounced once and hit the lowest branch of the tree. The umpire immediately signalled a four and put the bails in his pocket. We'd won with three overs to spare. Mack finished on a splendid 22 not out.

There was a bit of an argument over whether the Player of the Match was Clive or Mack but in the end we voted for Clive again. He was already the holder of the title following his fifty in the first game against Saracens.

...ipped. He suddenly charged down the pitch like a wild rhino
gave a huge heave and tried to hit the ball over the long-on
boundary. He missed completely and with his bat raised high he
turned to watch the keeper take off the bails.

HOME TEAM OLD BODILIANS V GLORY GARDENS	AWAY TEAM	AT OLD BODILIANS DATE AUGUST 31ST

INNINGS OF GLORY GARDENS .... TOSS WON BY O.B. WEATHER CLOUDY

BATSMAN	RUNS SCORED	HOW OUT	BOWLER	SCORE
1 M. ROSE	1·1·1·1·2·1·1·1	RUN	OUT	9
2 C. SEBASTIEN	1·1·1·1·2·2·1·3·2	bowled	BLACKETT-ORD	14
3 A. NAZAR	2·4·2	CT JESSY	BLACKETT-ORD	8
4 E. DAVIES		CT HAMILTON	BAGGINS	0
5 H. KNIGHT	1·2·2·6·2	CT FRIDAY	BAGGINS	13
6 C. DA COSTA	2·2·1·4·2·4·4·1·2·3·2·4·1·2	RUN	OUT	34
7 T. McCURDY	1·1·2·1·1·2·1·1·3·1·2·2·4	NOT	OUT	22
8 F. ALLEN	3·2·1·2	ST HAMILTON	BOOMER	8
9 T. VELLACOTT		bowled	BOOMER	0
10 J. GUNN	2	NOT	OUT	2
11 M. LEAR				

FALL OF WICKETS											BYES	2·1		3	TOTAL EXTRAS	12
SCORE	17	31	31	48	61	91	110	110	9	10	L BYES	1·2·1		4	TOTAL	122
BAT NO	2	3	4	5	1	6	8	9			WIDES	1·1·1		3	FOR	8
											NO BALLS	1·1		2	WKTS	

SCORE AT A GLANCE

BOWLER	BOWLING ANALYSIS : NO BALL + WIDE													OVS	MDS	RUNS	WKT
	1	2	3	4	5	6	7	8	9	10	11	12	13				
1 DE FRIEND	M	·:·	·:·	·:·	M	⊠	·2· 3·1·	+·2·1·3 4·1· ··1		⊠				8	2	23	0
2 BOOMER	·:·	M	M	3··	·:·1	⊠	·:· ··2	1·2 ww·04	2··					7·4	2	20	2
3 BAGGINS	··3 ···	+·+· ···	··· 2··	··· N·1	··· 0·1	··· ·2w	··2 ·21	M						8	1	19	2
4 BLACKETT-ORD	··2 w··	··· 1·2	4·2 ·w·	·2· 2··	·:· 1·6	M	4·· 2··	1·4 4··1	⊠					8	1	38	2
5 JESSY	··2 ···	··2 ···	··· 2··	·1· 1·3	·2· 2··									5	0	15	0
6																	
7																	
8																	
9																	

Chapter Six

On the bus home Frankie was unstoppable.

First he sang one of his silly Glory Gardens songs – although, as I've told you, "sang" isn't the word for what Frankie does. It began like this:

Glory Glory Gardens
Everybody knows us
We are the champions
Champions of the league.

And it went on and on all on the same note. In between the verses he made up little rhymes about each of the players in the team – his favourite was this one:

Frankie Allen
What a talent.
He's the keeper of your dreams
Moves like lightning
It's so fright'ning
For all the other teams.

At last the bus pulled in for us to get some fish and chips. Even Frankie stops singing while he's eating but as usual he was first to scoff down his food and he was soon begging everyone else to give him some of their chips.

"Clear off," said Cal through a mouthful of food, as Frankie leaned over and pinched his biggest chip.

"Mmmm . . . you don't understand," said Frankie. "I need more calories than you. It's all that extra energy I use up behind the stumps."

"Don't make me laugh, fatman," said Cal. "Why don't you look in the mirror. It's time you went on a diet."

"Good idea," said Jo. "But he's such a cheat he'd never stick to it."

Frankie ignored them. He wolfed down his stolen chip and looked round for someone else to prey on. Then his face suddenly brightened. "I bet Ohbert'll give me some of his fish. He only eats chips. Where is he?"

"On the back seat, sitting around collecting dust, I should think," said Tylan.

"And listening to his Walkman," said Azzie.

Frankie swaggered down the bus in search of Ohbert's supper. A moment later he was back. "He's not there." Frankie peered round at all the seats on the bus. "Has anybody hidden Ohbert anywhere?"

"Come to think of it, I didn't see him in the chippy," said Azzie.

"Maybe he's dematerialised," said Tylan.

"Don't be silly," said Jo. "I think we've left him behind. I knew there was a reason why Gatting didn't want to get on the bus." Gatting was still looking around anxiously and making little whining noises. "Look, he's trying to tell us that he's missing Ohbert."

Frankie went and told Kiddo, who was sitting up front next to the driver. "Who saw him last?" I asked.

"I think he was still in the shower when I came out," said Azzie.

"Maybe he slipped down the plughole," suggested Tylan.

"Shut up if you haven't got anything sensible to say," said Erica to Tylan angrily.

By now Kiddo was directing operations and looking very worried. He asked us all where we'd last seen Ohbert.

46

Meanwhile the bus turned round and we made our way back towards the Old Bodies' ground.

Tylan and Frankie were really enjoying the drama. "Kiddo'll probably go to prison for losing Ohbert," whispered Tylan.

"Great, no French next term," said Frankie. "But then who's going to complain about Ohbert going missing? His parents will probably give Kiddo a reward."

Both Erica and Jo were furious with them. "If you can't take this seriously, Francis Allen, there's no hope for you," said Jo to her brother.

"Why can't they grow up?" hissed Erica. "Poor Ohbert, who knows what has happened to him. He's probably starving and I bet he's got no money."

We passed the fish and chip shop, but there was no sign of Ohbert there. All of us, including Gatting, had our noses squashed against the windows to see who could spot him first.

At last the bus drove back into the cricket ground car park. All the cars had gone but in their place were two fire engines and a police car with its blue light flashing. Frankie led the charge out of the bus but Kiddo called him back and he told us to stay on board while he went to see what was going on. No-one took any notice and as soon as he and Gatting had disappeared into the pavilion we followed them.

Inside the strangest scene awaited us. There were three policemen, a policewoman, four firemen and, in the middle of them all, Ohbert. Gatting went straight up to Ohbert and gave him a big lick on the hand.

"Is he yours?" one of the policemen asked Kiddo. Kiddo nodded and then looked crossly at us as we all poured into the pavilion behind him.

The policeman continued. "He seems to have got himself locked in. He'd have been here all week if I hadn't happened to be walking past."

Ohbert opened his mouth to speak but nothing came out.

"From what I can make out, he fell asleep in the shower and, when he woke up, everyone had gone."

"Are you Mr Johnstone?" the policewoman asked Kiddo.

"Yes," said Kiddo, putting a hand on Ohbert's shoulder as if he was placing him under arrest. "It's entirely my fault. I should have counted them onto the bus. I can't tell you how glad I am to see him."

"I'm afraid we had to break in," said one of the firemen. "We thought he was a tramp or a vandal. You might get a bill for a broken window." Kiddo said he'd settle everything with Old Bodilians and, after he'd given the police his name and address, we all got back on the bus again. Ohbert waved goodbye to the firemen and we left for a second time.

"Old Bodilians will be dead pleased," said Cal. "First we give them a hiding and then the fire brigade smashes up their pavilion."

"And all to save Ohbert," said Azzie.

"How did you manage to fall asleep, Ohbert?" asked Erica.

"Oh, but I only just shut my eyes for a minute and then everyone was gone." Ohbert sniffed and rubbed his stomach. "Oh, but . . . I'm really hungry," he said.

"Let's stop at the chippy again," said Frankie. And a huge smile spread across his face. As we set off home for the second time another tuneless song echoed round the bus.

Ohbert Bennett
Missing person?
No he was just delayed.
He spent three hours
In the showers
With the cops and fire brigade.

———————— • ————————

It rained on Saturday so Nets were cancelled. Kiddo took us all for fitness training in the gym at school instead. The school had been painted slimy green in the holidays and it looked and smelt even more horrible than usual. It wasn't much fun knowing that we'd be back on Monday and the holidays were over.

We did some catching practice with a soft ball which was fun,

This is a good way to speed up your reactions for close to the wicket catches. You can do it with a soft or hard ball. The ball is thrown at the person with the bat from about five metres. The batter angles catches off the face of the bat towards the slip and gully cordon.

though not as good as proper Nets.

But mostly it was circuit training and jumping over "horses" and climbing ropes, which I don't enjoy much and Frankie really hates.

"What's the point of getting fit to play cricket?" he gasped, collapsing at the bottom of one of the ropes.

"It speeds up your reactions, kiddo," said Kiddo. "And your reactions cost us nine byes in the last game, not to mention the dropped catches and a missed stumping."

"So get up that rope, tubs," ordered Cal.

Frankie groaned. "I bet Jack Russell doesn't have to climb ropes."

"He's not 10 kilos overweight," said Cal.

"I promise I'll go on a diet if I can stop now," sighed Frankie.

"I want that in writing – with witnesses," said Cal. Frankie nodded feebly and with a sigh of relief he staggered off to change.

"I don't believe it," said Tylan. "Frankie on a diet! It doesn't sound quite right."

"I don't believe him," said Azzie. "Frankie'll wriggle out of it somehow."

"We'll see," said Cal.

When we finished training we found Frankie, already changed, sitting in a classroom and tucking into an extra long Mars bar.

"Banned," said Cal, snatching the Mars bar out of his mouth. Frankie's protests had no effect on Cal. "No diet, no final," he said. "That's the deal. You're going to lose at least two kilos before next Saturday or you won't be coming with us." We all nodded our agreement.

"There'll be a public weighing when we get home today," said Jo. "And then you'll have to stick to the rules if you want to play."

"What rules?"

"The rules of your diet. We're going to write them down for you," said Cal.

"You can't be serious," said Frankie aghast. He looked round desperately for support.

"But we are," I said.

"We're tired of having a slow, fat, unfit wicket-keeper," said Jacky.

"To make it more interesting for you," said Cal, "Kiddo's promised to give a fiver for every kilo you lose . . ."

Frankie sat up and suddenly looked interested. "Yeah?"

". . . to a charity of his choice."

He slumped back in his seat again, his hands nursing his stomach.

"Who's going to keep wicket for us next Saturday if Frankie doesn't make the weight?" asked Jacky.

"Azzie?" I suggested.

"I'll do it," said Mack.

Everyone was available for the final including Kris Johansen. We were allowed thirteen players in the squad – so Kris and even Ohbert would get at least one game each.

On the big day the games were all 20-over matches – it was the only way they could fit the programme into one day, said Jo. We had to play three games in our qualifying league and then the winners of each league would play off for the Champions League trophy. That was a lot of cricket even if we didn't make it to the final – so we'd probably be glad of the extra players even if one of them was Ohbert.

Kiddo told us we were going to Edgbaston on Friday evening and staying in a university college near the ground. "The first game's at 9.30 and we don't want anyone to be late," said Jo sternly.

"9.30! I might give that one a miss then," said Frankie who had already perked up a bit.

"You'll give them all a miss if you don't stick to this," said Cal. He had just finished writing out the rules of Frankie's diet. He handed them to Frankie.

THE F. ALLEN DIET

Rules

1. Breakfast. Cereal and one piece of thin toast. Definitely no fried potato.
2. Lunch. Jo will make you a packed lunch every day this week and you will not eat anything else.
3. You won't buy or scrounge anything between meals. That means no Mars bars, no crisps and definitely no chips.
4. After you have eaten tea (one helping only and you can't ask for more), you will not eat anything (except an apple if you are really hungry) for the rest of the day.
5. If you are caught breaking any of these rules you will be given one warning. If you do it again you will not play in the Champions League finals day.
6. You will also be banned from the Champions League if you haven't lost 2 kilos in weight by Saturday 10th September.

"Sign here," said Cal.

Frankie read and his mouth fell open in horror. He read it again. "You'll all be sorry you did this when I starve to death,"

51

he sighed. But after a lot of complaining and pleading, at last he signed and Jo put it carefully in her Glory Gardens folder which she takes with her everywhere.

"Can I have one last packet of barbecue crisps before I die?" asked Frankie feebly.

"No," we shouted with one voice.

Chapter Seven

Matthew Rose
Cal Sebastien
Azzie Nazar
Clive da Costa
Erica Davies
Hooker Knight
Mack McCurdy
Frankie Allen (if he's light enough)
Kris Johansen
Jacky Gunn
Marty Lear

Reserves: Tylan Vellacott
           Ohbert Bennett

"That's the team for the first game tomorrow," said Jo.

It had been a very hard decision to decide between Tylan and Kris but Ty made it easier for us by saying he'd stand down if we wanted to save a bowler. Kris is a good bowler and she can bat better than Tylan but I was a bit worried about losing the variation that his leg spin gives us. Jo had wanted Ohbert to play too, but in the end she agreed that we'd pick him for the second game.

"Looks like you'll be playing anyway, Ty," said Cal looking hard at Frankie's profile. "If he's lost two kilos I can't see which bit it's come off."

"You must be kidding," said Frankie. "I'm completely hollow. My stomach's been echoing since last Saturday. The only question is whether I'll have the strength to walk when I've got my pads on."

"When's the weigh-in?" asked Tylan.

"Tomorrow morning at the ground," said Cal. "There's bound to be a weighing machine at the county ground changing room."

"And it's going to cost Kiddo a fortune," said Frankie.

To be honest Frankie had been pretty good about the diet. He'd moaned a lot, of course, and Jo said she suspected he had been smuggling biscuits into his room at night because she'd found some crumbs in his bed. But we'd all kept a close eye on him and no-one had spotted him breaking the rules. I was really surprised that he'd lasted so long. Maybe it showed how much playing for Glory Gardens really means to him. But Cal was right – Frankie certainly didn't look any thinner. Perhaps it's impossible to lose two kilos in a week.

It wasn't only Frankie who had found it a long week. The first five days of the new term had been like an eternity. If it hadn't been for the Edgbaston final I don't think I would have survived. We got a fair bit of practice in after school in the evening and I spent most of the time in lessons thinking about tactics.

At last Friday afternoon came round and straight after the last lesson we piled into the school coach and set off for Birmingham.

We were staying in rooms in a college which Kiddo said was only just down the road from Edgbaston Cricket Ground. Two of the other teams playing in the final had arrived before us. They were called Edmondleigh and Langbottom.

The Langbottoms were friendly, noisy and cricket-mad – a bit like us. They wanted to know everything about Glory Gardens: where we came from, how we got our name, who was top of the batting and bowling averages. Frankie told them he was our best batsman and Matthew was our opening bowler. "Might as well confuse them a bit," he whispered.

One of the Langbottoms boasted that they were favourites to win the Champions League and, of course, that got Frankie going. In spite of his weakened state, he matched them boast for boast, telling them that he'd been first choice as the England Under 13 wicket-keeper but had to turn it down because of his commitment to Glory Gardens and the fact tht he had been so busy doing his Maths and English GCSEs two years early.

The Edmondleighs, meanwhile, kept themselves to themselves. They didn't really join in or say much. I couldn't decide whether it was because they were shy or that they just felt they were too good for us. Kiddo said he wished we could be as quiet and well behaved as they were.

The college was huge. Most of us had single rooms but Azzie and Marty were sharing and so were Frankie and Ohbert. Jo told Ohbert to make sure Frankie didn't eat anything in his room but if Ohbert understood what she was talking about he didn't show it. Cal said he'd already searched the room and Frankie's bags and he hadn't found any hidden packets of crisps or smuggled Mars bars.

"I'm very surprised and disappointed by your untrusting nature, Calvin," said Frankie adopting a hurt expression. During supper Frankie was unusually quiet and soon after he was the first to go off to bed.

"I'm worried about Frankie," said Mack. "I think this diet's taking some of the spirit out of him."

"Let's enjoy it while it lasts," said Cal.

"Don't be fooled. He's up to something," said Jo.

"How do you know?" I asked.

"Unfortunately I've lived with Francis all my life," said Jo. "And I just know when he's plotting something. I just wish I knew what it was."

We all went to bed quite early because Kiddo said we needed to get some rest before the big day. Breakfast was at 7.45am and the bus was leaving for Edgbaston at 8.30.

I couldn't sleep. I was lying in bed thinking about my plans for tomorrow when there was a tap at the door and in walked Cal.

"I thought you'd be awake," said Cal.

"I was thinking about the final."

"So was I."

Cal and I know each other so well that sometimes I think we can read each others minds. "Are we really going to drop Frankie if he doesn't go through the weight barrier?" he asked.

"Just what I was wondering."

"I think we should just give him a fright and then pick him anyway. It wouldn't really be fair to drop him just for being fat," said Cal.

"As long as it keeps him on his toes behind the stumps. He's missed a lot of chances lately," I said.

"That's mainly because he doesn't concentrate."

"I'm more worried about losing Tylan for the first game," I said.

"No problem, we've got six good bowlers – if you include me; that should be enough."

"There's not much variation though, apart from you – and me bowling left-arm."

"Perhaps you and Marty should open the bowling to mix it up a bit," suggested Cal.

We were still talking about our bowling attack when suddenly a high-pitched noise, half wail, half scream, tore through the building. It got louder and louder until it was unbearable.

"What is it?" I yelled sticking my fingers in my ears. Cal said something but I couldn't hear him, then he pointed to the door. We rushed out of the room together and found Kiddo in his pyjamas trying to round everyone up. Gatting was running up and down the corridor barking like a thing demented only you couldn't hear him either.

"I think it's the fire alarm, kiddo," shouted Kiddo in my ear. "Better get out of the building to be on the safe side."

By now the place was full of people running backwards and forwards, some in their pyjamas, some with towels round their waists. Gradually the panic died down and we all filed down the stairs and out through the front door of the building.

"It's raining," said Jacky.

"At least it'll put the fire out," said Tylan.

"What fire?" said Azzie. There certainly was no sign of a fire in the building – not even a puff of smoke.

Ohbert was the last to emerge from the college front door; he was wearing a long black nightgown.

"It's the Wizard of Oz," said Tylan.

"Oh but . . . Hooker. Have you seen Frankie?" asked Ohbert.

"Wasn't he in your room?"

"No but . . . I haven't seen him at all."

"Something fishy here," said Cal.

Once we were outside, no-one seemed to know what to do. So we just stood around getting wet and waiting for Kiddo to give us the all clear. After about five minutes the alarm stopped abruptly and at almost the same moment Kiddo appeared in the doorway firmly gripping Frankie's arm. "I think you can all go back to bed now. I'm afraid someone set off the burglar alarm in the kitchen."

"Francis? What were you doing . . ." began Jo.

"In the kitchen?" Cal demanded, adding, "As if we can't guess."

Frankie looked at us very sheepishly. "Er, I think I must have been sleepwalking."

"And sleep eating?" asked Cal.

"To bed, kiddoes," said Kiddo. "We'll talk about this in the morning if we're not all thrown out on the streets first by the management."

"I didn't eat a thing. Honest," said Frankie.

"We don't want to know, Francis," said Jo. "Go to bed. And don't move out of it until I tell you."

The Edmondleigh and Langbottom players filed back into the college, some grinning at Frankie, some scowling. We were all completely soaked to the skin.

"I don't think any of us are going to be much good tomorrow if we don't get some sleep," said Erica.

"I doubt we'll play at all," said Marty gloomily. "The ground'll be flooded."

I listened to the rain against my bedrooom window as I tried to go to sleep and, to be honest, I didn't feel any more optomistic than Marty.

Chapter Eight

The sun was shining at 8 o'clock the next morning when we filed into breakfast. Everyone looked dreadful.

"I hardly slept at all," complained Marty. "You should have heard Azzie snore."

Jacky sneezed. "What a great way to prepare for a cricket tournament," he said, looking accusingly at Frankie. "I think I've got pneumonia."

Breakfast was served. A plate of sausage, beans, bacon, egg and toast was placed in front of each of us. When it came to Frankie's turn Cal gave me a nudge and pointed to his plate. Frankie was staring in disbelief at a glass of orange juice and a single round of toast.

"What's this?"

"It's your breakfast," said Jo.

"Where is it? There isn't even any cereal," he moaned.

"They don't have cereal," said Jo sternly.

"Can't I have just one sausage." Frankie looked greedily at Marty's heaped plate next to him.

"Definitely not," said Jo. "After last night you're lucky to get any breakfast at all."

"Don't forget the weigh-in, fatman," said Cal.

"I won't have the strength to get on the scales," sighed Frankie.

Ohbert and Tylan missed breakfast completely. We found them both still asleep when we went back to the rooms. Kiddo said since they weren't playing, he'd bring them along as soon as

58

they were ready. The rest of us jumped on the bus and minutes later we drove into Edgbaston Cricket Ground.

"I bet this is exactly how the test match teams arrive," said Frankie peering out of the window of the bus. He had already livened up in spite of his empty stomach. "Look there's the Warwickshire flag. And I bet that's the indoor cricket school."

"I wonder if we'll see any of the players," said Matthew.

Eventually we found our way to the changing rooms. They were huge. A loud rumble from deep inside Frankie echoed around the walls. "I think I'm going to eat my wicket-keeping pads," he grumbled to himself.

"Better weigh in first," said Cal. He had found the weighing machine and he led Frankie over to face his moment of truth.

Frankie took a deep breath and stepped up. Cal looked closely at the dial and shook his head. "You haven't lost a microgram. If anything you're heavier than you were last week."

"Impossible," said Frankie. "The machine must be wrong." Then his face brightened and he started taking off his clothes.

"Whatever are you doing?"

"When I was weighed last Saturday I was in my shorts and I didn't have any shoes on."

As Frankie stripped Cal called out the weight. Off came his shirt, his trousers, his shoes, socks. Frankie was down to his underpants when Cal shouted, "Stop! That's it. Not quite two kilos but we've seen enough. Does everyone agree that Frankie plays?"

"Yes," we chorused.

"Thank goodness for that," said Frankie. And with a grin he picked up one of his cricket boots and pulled a Mars bar out of it. He'd eaten it before anyone could stop him.

When we'd changed Jo returned with the programme for the day.

"Thimbledown are the favourites," said Jo. "So we've got the hardest league. Cherrystanton and Edmondleigh are the best teams in League A."

"How do you know?" I asked.

"I've been talking to people," said Jo importantly.

"Langbottom fancy themselves, too," said Azzie.

"At least they'll be as tired as we are," said Marty, yawning as he spoke.

Jacky sneezed. "I hope they've all got colds, too."

We walked out to look at the pitch. It was enormous.

"Second largest test ground in England after the Oval," said Matthew who knows about that sort of thing. "I think it's nearly 170 yards across the widest bit.

The ground had been divided into two pitches; each of them looked at least as big as the Priory Ground. The boundaries were marked by ropes and two score-boards had been set up in the middle between the pitches. We were playing on the one right in front of the pavilion. The umpires were already out putting up the stumps.

As usual, we relied on Jo to tell us exactly what was going on. "Edmondleigh and Cherrystanton are playing on the far pitch," she explained. "And the other two games are on the practice ground behind the big score-board."

I found the Langbottom captain and we went out to the middle to toss up.

"How's your wicket-keeper this morning?" he asked. "Still sleepwalking?" Asad Butt was typical of the whole Langbottom team – brimful of confidence and enthusiasm. You could see that the idea of losing to us hadn't even crossed his mind. Right, I thought, you're in for a big shock. Asad won the toss and he took no time in deciding to bat.

"Get your pads on," he shouted to his two openers. "And don't come back until you've both got a century."

As the Glory Gardens players streamed on to the field I saw Tylan, Ohbert and Kiddo arrive and take their seats in the front of the pavilion. Tylan gave me a "thumbs up".

After padding up, Frankie came out with the Langbottom openers. "You're not batting without helmets, are you?" he said to them. "That's a bit risky against our bowlers."

I decided to ignore Cal's advice and stick to the regular

60

CHAMPIONS LEAGUE

League A	League B
Round 1.	
Edmondleigh v Cherrystanton	Glory Gardens v Langbottom
Elphinstone Forest v Bishops Ardley	Cragg Moor v Thimbledown
Round 2.	
Bishops Ardley v Edmondleigh	Thimbledown v Glory Gardens
Cherrystanton v Elphinstone Forest	Langbottom v Cragg Moor
Round 3.	
Cherrystanton v Bishops Ardley	Cragg Moor v Glory Gardens
Edmondleigh v Elphinstone Forest	Thimbledown v Langbottom

Final

Winner of League A v Winner of League B
(for the winner and runner-up of the Champions Cup)

Runner-up of League A v Runner-up of League B
(play-off for third and fourth positions)

opening attack of Marty and Jacky. I could see that my left-arm bowling would offer some variety but I didn't want to break up a winning partnership.

To begin with both bowlers were completely out of form. Marty's first two overs were all over the place and Jacky just couldn't find his length. It was probably just the pressure of the big occasion but I was also beginning to believe that Jacky really was getting sick. Either way Langbottom got off to a flier. After four overs they had 21 on the board and I was already thinking of a bowling change. Then Marty suddenly got one to nip back off the pitch and over went the opener's off-stump. That brought Asad Butt, their captain, to the wicket.

I'd had a feeling from the moment I met Asad that he could bat – something about the way he moved reminded me of Azzie, Liam Katz and other top batsmen I've seen. I wasn't wrong. He got off the mark with a sweetly timed pull through mid-wicket and from that moment he hardly put a foot wrong.

In spite of last night's heavy rain the outfield was lightning fast and we were soon chasing the ball all over the ground. Fortunately for us Erica took a brilliant catch high over her head in the covers to dismiss the other opener and then Marty popped up again with a smart caught and bowled. His four overs cost 20 runs however and, as he and Jacky came to the end of their spells, Langbottom had 37 on the board and Asad was at full throttle.

I turned to Erica to stem the flow of runs. She's the ideal limited-overs bowler to have in your side; she's always a hundred per cent accurate and most batters find it difficult to get after her.

Asad drove Erica for four off her first ball but she didn't panic and even he could do nothing with the next five balls except play them back defensively.

I decided it was time for me to come on at the other end. I bowled left-arm over the wicket and tried to vary my length and pace to unsettle the batsmen. Their No. 5 played and missed at a ball which swung across him outside the off-stump. Then I had him plumb lbw, only the umpire called no ball. A single down the leg side brought Asad on strike. He clipped me off his legs for two but then I nearly had him with a shooter which went under his bat and skimmed by the off-stump. The ball bounced a second time in front of Frankie and popped up and hit him in the mouth.

The damage wasn't serious but he had a small cut on his bottom lip which bled a bit, so we stopped for repairs. Kiddo came on with his first-aid kit and Jo brought out a drink of water for her brother. Frankie made the most of the drama as usual. "Water, water," he groaned, taking the glass from Jo.

"If you'd concentrate this sort of thing wouldn't happen, Francis," said Jo, realising that Frankie wasn't really hurt.

"I thought I'd try catching it in my mouth for a change," said Frankie. "It gets boring using the gloves all the time."

Cal took advantage of the break to come over for a quiet word with me. "We've got to try and keep their skipper away from the bowling," he said. "He's scoring too fast."

"I know that. Got any ideas?"

"Drop the field back for him and give him a single and then tighten

The grubber or shooter is a wicket-keeper's nightmare. Frankie is not in position for the second bounce and, if the ball bounces awkwardly, he'll have problems covering it.

The best approach to a shooter is to stand up and get both your pads in line; then bend and take the ball in front of them. The pads should be together and inclined forward so that if you miss the ball with your gloves your head and body are protected.

up again for the other batter. That way he'll have to try and hit boundaries or lose the strike."

I thought for a moment. Maybe I should bring Cal on. If you're going to score boundaries off slow bowlers you have to really hit the ball – and that always gives the bowler a chance.

"You're on next over at my end," I said. Even though I'd bowled only one over I decided it was worth experimenting.

Frankie was on his feet again and grinning away, though now it was a rather odd grin because his bottom lip was twice as big as his top one.

I kept the field in close for Erica and we managed to keep Asad away from the strike for a whole over. Just two runs came off it from a slice past gully.

Cal came on to a very defensive field.

"This will have them in two minds," said Frankie. "They won't know whether to hit him for a six or a four."

I passed the word around that everyone should be on their toes to stop the second run. Asad took an easy single off the first ball and the fielders immediately closed in.

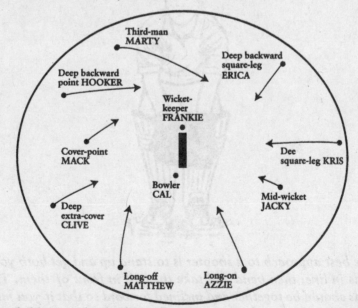

The field moves in for the tail-ender.

64

Frankie spoiled the plan slightly by letting the next ball through his legs for two byes to bring up Langbottom's fifty. Cal was furious with him. "Listen, fatlip, it'll be your nose next time if you don't concentrate," he said.

Frankie shrugged but he looked rather hurt.

After that things improved a bit. We kept their skipper away from the bowling for the rest of the over and, when I moved the field out again for the last ball, they took the single which kept him off strike for Erica's next over, too.

The two batsmen met in the middle. I knew Asad had spotted what we were up to and I was wondering what he'd do to counter it. It wasn't long before we found out.

The first ball of Erica's next over was well pitched up and the batsman dropped it down in front of him and shot off for a run. Asad was backing up and he was well in when Clive's direct shy hit the stumps. Back went the field. Now Asad picked out Matthew, who's not the quickest fielder in the game. He didn't hit the ball hard to him but just glanced it softly down to long-leg and they ran two.

"Wake up, Matt. On the single," I shouted.

Next ball Asad tried the same trick. He ran the ball in the direction of Kris at deep extra-cover but she was too quick for him. He started the second run and then screamed, "No," when he saw Kris had the ball in her hands. Her throw was right over the stumps and he'd have been miles out if he'd taken her on.

Erica bowled out the rest of the over without giving away another run. The score-board stood at 55 for three. The number of overs remaining went up as I watched – 7. I knew Asad had to take a few chances now and I strengthened the mid-wicket area, moving Marty from third-man.

"Are you setting your field for my bad ball?" joked Cal.

"Keep it on the spot. He's got to go for boundaries, now," I said.

Asad went for the gap at third-man with a reverse sweep and took two runs. Cal gave the next ball a lot more air and he swung on the leg side straight to Kris at backward square-leg. There was an easy single but they didn't take it. The third ball was driven straight over Cal's head for four, but it dropped only yards away from Azzie at long-on. He was taking risks all right . . . and so far it was paying off.

Three balls of the over remained. Would Asad take the single now or go for another boundary? He came down the pitch to Cal who saw him coming at the last minute and fired the ball in short. Asad swung at it and missed and Frankie took the ball cleanly and flicked off the bails.

"Fatlip, I forgive you," said Cal rushing towards Frankie with his arms in the air. "What a stumping!"

"It was nothing," said Frankie. "Just pure genius."

We clapped off the Langbottom captain; he'd scored 27 out of his team's 61.

I saw Tylan and Jo cheering us from the pavilion and gave them a wave. They'd realised too that we'd got rid of the main threat. Now we had to keep things tight for the next six overs. Erica continued the job with a final over that cost only three runs. She finished with fine figures again – four overs for 13 runs – having snuffed out the Langbottom run chase brilliantly. But now her spell was over and I had to find another bowler to take over at her end.

Cal continued at the other but he seemed to lose concentration for a time and it cost us two fours – one of them nearly a six. At the end of his over I was still hesitating over whom to bring on next – me or Kris Johansen? I didn't know much about her bowling or how she'd perform under pressure but I decided to risk her. The first over was a bit of a mixture. She twice beat the bat but then she fired in a couple of loose ones down the leg side, one was struck for three the other went for four wides. Suddenly, in the space of two overs, the score had leapt into the eighties and we were back on the defensive again.

Cal bowled out the 18th and his last over – it went for five runs. Then Kris came back with the perfect reply. A fast yorker practically cut the batsman in half and hammered into his leg stump. 85 for five.

The new batsman was beaten for pace by the first two balls he received. The second of them was too fast for Frankie as well and it went for two more byes.

I came on again for the last over of the innings. The field was set well back and they scrambled four runs off my first three balls, one of them a leg-bye. Then they took one risk too many, chancing a single on Mack's throw. The ball whizzed in at stump height and Frankie had plenty of time to flick off the bails. I clean bowled the incoming batsman with the last ball of my over and they finished their twenty overs on 93 for seven.

It had been an up and down sort of performance but I was reasonably pleased. As Marty said, it wasn't a disaster. Of course, being Marty, he thought we had little chance of scoring the runs. 94 was a long haul, even with a fast outfield. But we simply had to win against Langbottom because our next game was against Thimbledown, the favourites.

HOME TEAM	LANGBOTTOM	V	GLORY GARDENS	AWAY TEAM	AT EDGBASTON!
					DATE SEPTEMBER 10

INNINGS OF ...LANGBOTTOM...   TOSS WON BY LANG. WEATHER SUNNY

BATSMAN	RUNS SCORED	HOW OUT	BOWLER	SCORE
1 D. GORDON	2·1·1·2·2 》 — —— —— —··	bowled	LEAR	8
2 C. PARKER	3·2·4·1·1·1 》 — —— — — —	CT DAVIES	GUNN	12
3 ASAD BUTT	2·1·2·4·1·1·4·2·1·2·1·2·4 》—	ST ALLEN	SEBASTIEN	27
4 J. LACKLAND	》· — — — — — ·· — —	c&b	LEAR	0
5 J. HODGES	1·1·2·1·1·1·1·4·4·1·1 》· · — —	bowled	JOHANSEN	18
6 C. HAWKINS	1·3·2·2·2 — — — — · —	NOT	OUT	10
7 R. TANCRED	2·1 》 — — ·· — · —	RUN	OUT	3
8 T. BALDWIN	》 · · — — — · · ·	bowled	KNIGHT	0
9 S. ROLLINS	· — — — —			
10 B. BIGARD	— — ·· —			
11 A. KHILJI				

FALL OF WICKETS											BYES	1·2·2 — —— ····—	5	TOTAL EXTRAS	15
SCORE	22	27	34	61	85	93	93	8	9	10	L BYES	1·1	2	TOTAL	93
	1	2	3	4	5	6	7				WIDES	1·1·1·4	7	FOR	
BAT NO	1	2	4	3	5	7	8				NO BALLS	1	1	WKTS	7

SCORE AT A GLANCE

BOWLER	BOWLING ANALYSIS · NO BALL + WIDE													OVS	MDS	RUNS	WKT
	1	2	3	4	5	6	7	8	9	10	11	12	13				
1 M. LEAR	··2 ·3	4··1 +·11	·1W +·2·	2·4 ··W	✕									4	0	20	2
2 J. GUNN	·2· 4··	··2 ·2·	··1· 1W·	1·1· 1·1	✕									4	0	15	1
3 E. DAVIES	4·· ···	·· 2··	·21 ···	1·· 11·	✕									4	0	13	0
4 H. KNIGHT	··· 012·	✕	·21 ··W											2	0	7	1
5 C. SEBASTIEN	··1 ··1	2·4· W··	·4·1· ·4·	··1· 2·2	✕									4	0	21	1
6 K. JOHANSEN	··3 ···1	W·· ··2												2	0	10	1
7																	
8																	
3																	

Chapter Nine

"Don't forget the singles," I reminded Matthew and Cal as they went out to open the Glory Gardens' innings.

Matthew knew what I was getting at. We needed a good start and we couldn't afford another dead-bat performance from him.

Asad Butt opened the bowling at the big score-board end and it didn't take a fortune-teller to see that we had a real fight on our hands. He was quick and straight.

A short ball reared on Matthew and hit him in the chest. "Ouch, that hurt," said Tylan.

"It's his height," said Mack. "He's getting more bounce than we did."

"The trouble is Jacky and Marty are just too short," said Frankie. "They need to put on some growth. Plenty of manure – and maybe a week on the rack just to stretch them a bit."

"Wouldn't it be easier to get Cal to bowl fast instead? He's tall enough," said Tylan.

It wasn't just Asad who was bowling well. The other opener was fairly hostile too and Matthew and Cal did well to survive. Asad had a brilliant change of pace and his quick ball was genuinely fast. Matthew was hit again; a nasty blow on the arm this time but, if he was hurt he didn't show it. After five overs "leg-byes" was the highest scorer – the total had limped to 15.

It wasn't the bowlers who ended the opening partnership however, but a brilliant throw from the long-leg boundary.

Matthew played a very fine leg glance and it looked like an easy two. He may have hesitated a bit on the turn but the pick-up and throw from the boundary was in Mack's class. Even then only a direct hit would have beaten Matthew, but hit it did and he was run out for the second time in succession.

"No need for the third umpire for that one," said Tylan. The first wicket had gone down with the score on 17.

A few moments later a ball from Asad reared on Cal and he just couldn't get his glove out of the way. It lobbed to slip and Cal was on his way back, too.

Clive announced his arrival at the crease with a classic back-foot drive. Then all of a sudden the opening attack had completed their eight overs and Azzie and Clive were facing two spinners – one right-arm and one left – and it was a different game. Having put all the pressure on with the quickies, Asad immediately went on the defensive. It was as if he was saying, "Right, if you want the runs, come and get them."

Both Azzie and Clive are naturally attacking players and, of course, their response was to hit out. But with the fielders on the boundary there weren't too many gaps. Azzie found one with a fierce pull that bounced once before crossing the rope but mostly, even though they were hitting the ball hard, the runs came in singles. At the half way point we had reached 35. That meant we needed nearly six an over from now on. Things didn't get any easier when Clive fell to a good catch on the mid-wicket boundary.

"Take the singles and give Azzie the strike," I instructed Erica.

The tension was becoming unbearable as Langbottom turned the screw. I had never felt anything like it – not in the League nor in the Colts games. I knew this was the big one and the thought of losing was giving me a sick feeling in the pit of my stomach.

Still the Langbottom tactics continued to pay off. Erica was pushing the singles but Azzie wasn't finding the boundaries we needed. Time and again beautifully timed cuts, drives and pulls went straight to the fielders. The overs ticked by and I could feel the game slipping away from us. And I didn't know what to do about it.

"46 for three. Seven overs remaining," shouted Jo to us. We

watched the number 7 go up on the score-board.

"If Azzie can't hit a boundary no-one can," said Marty gloomily.

"Let me at them," said Frankie swinging his bat. "A couple of sixes will put us back in it."

Azzie was trying his best – we could all see that. An enormous cheer went up when at last a four screamed across the square-leg boundary. But there was an even bigger cheer from the Langbottoms next ball, as Azzie top-edged and the bowler ran towards mid-wicket to take a skier over his shoulder. It was a brilliant catch and Azzie tapped him on the back in approval as he walked off.

53 for four and I was in.

"Relax. No need to go mad," said Erica who had walked out to meet me. "We need 40 in six overs. That shouldn't be beyond us with all that batting to come."

I nodded. But I kept thinking, we need boundaries, singles won't do. I got off the mark with a skied leg-side swing which dropped just short of the fielder on the mid-wicket boundary. Then I drove the second ball straight back along the ground to the bowler. I must hit the next one, I thought.

The spinner flighted a slower ball and I took a pace down the pitch and went for it. If I'd got to the pitch it would have been a straight six. But I didn't. The ball shot high in the air off an outside edge and the lone cover fielder close in on the off side had plenty of time to run round and take the catch. I'd faced three balls and made our position worse rather than better. I was really ashamed of myself.

Mack was clean bowled first ball, swinging with his head in the air.

"That's 56 for five," said Jo. She looked rather suspiciously at Frankie who was about to bound out to the crease. "Surprise us, Francis," she said. "Don't close your eyes and swing at everything."

"Relax," said Frankie. "I'm in control."

The second of the two spinners had only five balls to bowl.

If you're going to attack a spinning ball off the front foot, the first rule is "get to the pitch". If you don't, and the ball turns as it does here, you'll either miss it completely or edge a catch.

Frankie played and missed at the first with a huge swoosh. It was only after he had played it that Jo told us it was a hat-trick ball. The awfulness of the shot seemed to calm Frankie down and he followed up with a couple of good drives.

To my dismay Asad now brought on another spinner – a leggie this time. Frankie has a good chance of knocking a couple of boundaries against medium pacers because he's got such a good eye. But spinners are his weakness – he thinks they're easy and he forgets to move his feet.

Two wild air shots were met with groans of disbelief from the Glory Gardens bench but then, at last, Frankie got one in the middle of the bat and it bounced just short of the mid-wicket boundary and went for four in spite of the fielder's despairing lunge.

A medium pacer came on at the other end. With three overs to go we still needed 27 – nine runs an over. If only Frankie could clout a couple more fours we'd be back in the chase. However, it was Erica who posted the next boundary with a delicate sweep played very fine which beat both the keeper and the fielder running round at long-leg.

With two overs left we were still 20 short of our target. Again Frankie connected with the big heave against the spinner and again the ball eluded the fielder and went for four.

"It must be the diet," said Cal. "Come on, slim. You can do it." Frankie waved his bat and then played a deft little glide on the off side for a single. But we all knew, Frankie included, that singles wouldn't win us the match. Erica went for a straight drive over the bowler's head but the boundary fielders cut off the four and again we could only manage one run.

Frankie eyed the leg-side boundary greedily. The leg spinner bowled just outside off-stump and turning away. Frankie swung across the line and there was an audible snick and a cry of delight from the keeper as he held the ball up high. Frankie had gone for 12 to the last ball of the nineteenth over.

"Thirteen to win, Kris," said Jo. It had crossed my mind for a moment to send Marty in instead of Kris because he's probably a harder hitter of the ball – but I ruled it out. Erica was on strike and, if we were going to win, she had to do it for us. The Langbottoms were anxiously organising their field placings for the two girls who were deep in discussion in the middle of the pitch. I hadn't given Kris any instructions. They both knew what they had to do.

At last Erica faced up to the medium pacer and she cut him away fine of deep point for two. Another fierce cut went straight to the boundary fielder who was backing up well and they could only manage a single.

"That's it," said Marty gloomily.

"Shut up, misery," said Frankie and then he jumped and cheered the umpire for giving a wide for a ball down the leg side.

"Shut up, Frankie," said Kiddo without even looking at him.

Four balls remained and we needed nine to win. Kris managed to paddle a short one away for a single and Erica was back on strike. As the bowler delivered she stepped across her stumps and swung the ball from outside the off to the square-leg boundary. It was so beautifully timed that the fielder wasn't in the race. Two balls left and four to win. It was getting unbearable. Erica and Kris met in the middle again. My guess was that Erica was telling her to run two if the ball didn't go for four.

This time Erica stepped back outside her leg stump and cut hard. She was a bit off-balance as she played the shot and nearly fell over before scampering off down the wicket. The ball was in the fielder's hands as she turned. "Yes," she cried and went for the second run.

"Let the throw be wide," I whispered to myself. But it was low and hard. It came in on the bounce and the wicket-keeper appealed as he demolished the stumps. Up went the square-leg umpire's finger.

Marty was ready. I'd told him to go in ahead of Jacky. "Three to win, two to tie," said Jo.

"Go for the big one, Mart," said Frankie. "Death or Glory."

The Langbottoms were now every bit as excited as we were. Asad was trying to place his field around the boundary and everyone in the team was getting in on the act and making suggestions to him. Even the wicket-keeper had gone back twenty paces to cut off the lucky snick.

At last the bowler ran in and bowled a yorker on middle stump. Marty gave it the full monty and missed completely. Over went his wicket.

"Blast," said Kiddo. Then he looked at the dejected faces around him and quickly added. "That was close, kiddoes. We'll just have to win the next one, won't we?"

HOME TEAM	LANGBOTTOM	V	GLORY GARDENS	AWAY TEAM	AT EDGBASTON DATE SEPTEMBER 10th

INNINGS OF GLORY GARDENS.......... TOSS WON BY LANG.. WEATHER SUNNY.

	BATSMAN	RUNS SCORED	HOW OUT	BOWLER	SCORE
1	M.ROSE	1·1·1	RUN	OUT	3
2	C.SEBASTIEN	1·1·2·2·1	CT HODGES	ASAD BUTT	7
3	A.NAZAR	1·1·1·4·1·1·1·1·1·1·1·4	C & b	HODGES	19
4	C.DACOSTA	2·2·1·1·1	CT KHILJI	BIGARD	7
5	E.DAVIES	1·1·1·1·1·1·1·1·1·1·1·2·1·1·4·1·1·1 2·1·4·1	RUN	OUT	31
6	H.KNIGHT	1	CT PARKER	BIGARD	1
7	T.McCURDY		bowled	HODGES	0
8	F.ALLEN	1·1·4·1·4·1	CT TANCRED	KHILJI	12
9	K.JOHANSEN	1	NOT	OUT	1
10	M.LEAR		bowled	BALDWIN	0
11	J.GUNN				

FALL OF WICKETS														BYES	---------	-	TOTAL EXTRAS	10
		1	2	3	4	5	6	7	8	9	10							
SCORE		17	19	36	53	56	56	81	91	91			LBYES	1·2·1·1·2		7	TOTAL	91
BAT NO		1	2	4	3	6	7	8	5	10			WIDES	1·1·1		3	FOR	
													NO BALLS		-		WKTS	9

SCORE AT A GLANCE

	BOWLER	BOWLING ANALYSIS : NO BALL ⚬ WIDE													OVS	MDS	RUNS	WKT
		1	2	3	4	5	6	7	8	9	10	11	12	13				
1	ASAD BUTT	1··	·1·	2··	·11 w·2	✕									4	0	8	1
2	S. ROLLINS	··1	1···	·2	·+·· ··2	✕									4	0	9	0
3	B. BIGARD	··+1 1·4	·W·1 1·1	·1· 1·1	·11 1·W	✕									4	0	18	2
4	J. HODGES	1·1 ·11	1·1 ·1	·1· 1·W	W·1 ··1	✕									4	0	18	2
5	A.KHILJI	2·1 ··4	1·4 1·W												2	0	14	1
6	T. BALDWIN	11·· 4·1	21+1 W·1W												2	0	16	1
7																		
8																		
9																		

Chapter Ten

"**M**aybe we shouldn't play Ohbert in the next game, after all," suggested Marty.

"Will you never learn?" said Jo to Marty with a sad shake of the head. "Maybe we should leave you out after that terrible shot in the last game."

Jo, Marty and I were picking the team for our next match against Thimbledown, the London champions and hot favourites. We both knew exactly what Jo was talking about. Glory Gardens had been nearly blown apart earlier in the season because of dropping Ohbert. There'd been a huge row and Marty walked out and even playing against us – for our arch-enemy, Wyckham Wanderers. There were some in the team who hadn't forgiven him yet for that dreadful act of treachery.

"Just a suggestion," said Marty backing off quickly. "Forget I said it."

"I should think so," Jo smiled. "So we agree that Kris and Matthew will stand down for Tylan and Ohbert?"

Marty and I nodded. We also decided to experiment with Azzie as an opener because of the need for quick runs early in the innings.

We joined the others who were sitting in the front row of seats at the Press Box end of the ground, waiting for the next game to start.

As I expected Matthew was very disappointed when I told him he'd been dropped but I promised him he'd be back for the third qualifying game.

This was the team in batting order:

Azzie Nazar
Cal Sebastien
Clive da Costa
Erica Davies
Hooker Knight
Mack McCurdy
Frankie Allen
Tylan Vellacott
Jacky Gunn
Marty Lear
Ohbert Bennett

"Cherrystanton trounced Edmondleigh in the other game on the main ground," said Tylan. Cherrystanton are the Somerset champions and Jo's tip for the final.

The second game on the far pitch had already started. We'd drawn the pitch at the Press Box end this time for our game against Thimbledown. In front of us the Thimbledown team was doing a lot of weird warming-up exercises, instructed by a blond, ultra-fit-looking man in a track suit who I guessed was their games teacher. He had a very loud and unpleasant voice.

"Does anyone know how Thimbledown got on in their first game?" I asked.

"No. They've been too busy for us to ask them," said Jacky. "Who were they playing?"

"Cragg Moor," said Jo. "But it's a strange thing, I don't think I've seen the Cragg Moor team. I've only counted seven sides so far."

"Maybe they're too scared to show up . . . like the Aussies in the World Cup," said Frankie with a wink at Mack.

He wasn't that far from the truth because moments later Kiddo arrived with the news that the Cragg Moor side hadn't arrived and they were out of the tournament. "I can't think what's happened but it's rotten luck. Just think how you'd feel,

77

kiddoes, if it was us."

"Terrible. Does that mean we get four points for beating them?" said Frankie insensitively.

"Even if we do, so will everyone else, dumbo," said Jo.

"So Thimbledown haven't played yet," I said.

"Right, kiddo."

"You know what that means," said Marty.

"What?" I asked.

"Just that we've got no chance of qualifying now."

"Oh, of course not," said Frankie. "We may as well go and put our heads in the oven or jump off the pavilion roof. Come on everyone, follow me. We'll commit team suicide."

"It means," said Jo. "That if we beat Thimbledown and they beat Langbottom, we can still go through on run difference or wickets or whatever the rules of the competition are.

"You mean you don't know," teased Frankie. "That's not like you, Jo, is it?"

"I'll find out," said Jo crossly.

This time I won the toss. The Thimbledown skipper hardly spoke to me and his cold expression gave nothing away when I told him that we would bat. His team took the field and immediately they went into another huddle around their blond trainer.

"Concentrate with every ball . . . You know you're the better team . . ." I heard him bark. "Keep pressurising them . . . Play for each other . . . Appeal together and make sure the umpire hears you." He went on and on. I supposed it was his way of psyching up the players.

"I thought Kiddo was bad," said Frankie. "But he doesn't give us any of that old rubbish. Knock them all over the ground, Az, my boy. That'll show them."

In the short time since we'd met the Thimbledown players, we hadn't discovered many of their good points. As Azzie and Cal set off for the middle, there was an air of grim determination growing in the Glory Gardens camp.

"I hope Azzie's saved up a big one for this lot," said Jacky, before going into another fit of sneezes.

"Relax," said Frankie. "Glory Gardens will see them off. I've got a feeling about this one."

"We'd better win," said Matthew. "Because I want another game."

Thimbledown opened their bowling with a spinner. Azzie went to sweep his second ball which looked as if it was going down the leg side. He didn't get hold of it and the ball hit his front pad. There was a huge appeal and Azzie smiled but the smile left his face as he saw the umpire slowly raising his finger. He turned rather slowly and walked.

Azzie was still telling us how he had got a snick on to his pad and anyway it was missing the leg stump by miles when Clive played on. He got a ball that kept a bit low outside the off-stump and cut it on to his stumps. We were 0 for two and our two best batsmen were back in the changing room.

A big crowd of Thimbledown supporters over to our left was going wild. It seemed to be mostly made up of the players' parents but the blond trainer was in the middle of them shouting instructions. "Fine bowling, Foxy. Don't let them off the hook now," he rasped.

You could feel the state of shock in the Glory Gardens team. Erica got up grimly and strode out to bat without saying a word. She didn't have to face because it was the end of the over. Cal played out a maiden from the other end against a nippy bowler with a fast arm action.

Then the spinner bowled again.

"He's not even turning it," said Tylan.

We cheered the first runs of our innings as if we'd just seen Erica bring up her fifty with a six – in fact, it was a neat cover drive for two. Slowly Erica and Cal started to repair the damage, cautiously at first, then with growing confidence. Cal pulled the spinner for two to take us into double figures. Next ball he took a step forward to drive and missed. He immediately swung round and grounded his bat and from the boundary it seemed that he'd beaten the stumping attempt which wasn't the quickest

I'd ever seen.

Again there was an enormous appeal from the whole Thimbledown team and the square-leg umpire gave it out without a second's thought. Their wicket-keeper captain, threw the ball in the air with a shout of triumph as he was mobbed by the rest of his team.

"That was never . . ." Jacky's sentence was cut short by another resounding sneeze.

"Of course it wasn't. He was in by miles," shouted Frankie.

I think the umpire heard him because he glared at us and Kiddo told Jacky and Frankie to keep their opinions to themselves. He didn't say they were wrong, though.

I suddenly realised I was in and got to my feet. I certainly didn't feel too well prepared for my innings which was starting a lot earlier than I expected.

"10 for three," said Azzie. "Time for a captain's knock."

It was the second time I'd joined Erica in the middle in scarcely an hour. "Welcome again," she said. "Slightly different problem this time, I think. What's the plan?"

"Score fifty and keep going," I said and I took guard. Tylan was right, the spinner wasn't turning it. Yet somehow he'd taken three wickets — with a little help from both the umpires. I told myself not to think about that. Runs were what mattered and Erica and I had to score them. I concentrated hard and was off the mark with the third ball I faced — a little push into the covers. A few balls later I got a juicy long hop from the spinner and pulled him away for four.

"The keeper's doing a lot of talking," said Erica when we met again in the middle at the end of the over.

"Funny that, he didn't say a word when we tossed up," I said.

"He's keen on appealing, too," said Erica. "He even appeals for lbw when you hit the ball in the middle of the bat. I just hope the umpires realise he's trying it on."

Soon I began to settle down and enjoy myself. A new pair of bowlers took over — accurate, medium pacers but otherwise nothing too special. By the half way stage Erica and I had pushed the score up to 29 for three. Now we needed to start to accelerate.

Erica flicked one on the off side and called me for a quick single. I was backing up a long way and slid my bat in well before the throw whizzed past the stumps. The keeper hadn't got up in time to collect it and the ball bounced away down to deep square-leg. I turned, called for the overthrow and ran.

Then I saw Erica and stopped. She had run way past the wicket at the bowler's end. She turned and saw me half way down the pitch and set off for the second run. I caught a glimpse of the retrieving fielder picking up the ball and I knew right away it was going to be close. I ran my bat in and turned to see Erica diving for the line and the bails flying in the air.

I couldn't tell whether she was in or out but there seemed to be no doubt in their captain's mind. He bellowed another huge appeal and went on a run of celebration. Although he took a bit more time to think about it this time, the square-leg umpire raised his finger.

Erica picked herself and her bat up and walked off, leaving me alone to reflect whether or not it had been my fault.

Mack thought the run out had been a close call. "We don't seem to be getting the benefit of the doubt much today, mate," he said breezily as he passed me – loud enough for the umpire and the Thimbledowns to hear. Then he dropped his voice: "What are the orders then?"

"Give me as much of the strike as you can," I said.

"Be ready to run," he said.

Mack immediately dropped the first ball at his feet and called me through for a cheeky but safe single. I cracked the next delivery through the covers for four.

Their skipper made another bowling change and took ages rearranging his field. The new bowler was a slow left-hander and he bowled from round the wicket with the umpire standing up. His first ball deceived me a bit in the air and I played and missed. "Howzthaaaaat?" The keeper-captain went up for the catch.

"Rubbish," I rounded on him with an angry glare. "I was

nowhere near it and you know it." Fortunately this time the umpire agreed with me. Not only that, he walked down the pitch and had a word about "silly appeals". The Thimbledown skipper went bright red and nodded but he was soon at it again when a ball down the leg side hit Mack on the pad. Again the umpire shook his head. Then Mack, to his great annoyance, got a leading edge and the bowler snaffled the return catch like Frankie with a plateful of sausages. And that brought Frankie himself to the wicket.

"This Scott person likes the sound of his own voice, doesn't he?" said Frankie hypocritically.

"Scott, is that the captain's name?" I asked.

"Yeah he's down in the book as G. Scott. I think the G's for Great."

Frankie's first scoring shot, off his first ball, was a top edge which just cleared the fly slip and we ran two.

In the next over I leg-glanced the ball straight to fine-leg and, for reasons only he understood, Frankie called me through for a single. It would have been suicide even for a fast runner between wickets like Azzie, but for Frankie it was plain ridiculous. He slouched off, run out by nearly half the length of the pitch. Tylan survived one lbw shout and fell to the second.

Now we'd slumped again, to 43 for seven with only Jacky, Marty and Ohbert to come. The Thimbledown players and their supporters were delirious – you'd have thought they'd already won from the way they were strutting about. I took a deep gulp of air and then breathed out slowly. We needed 60 or 70 to have a chance and now it was all up to me.

Jacky took a leg-bye off the last ball of the over and kept me away from the strike. We now had six overs left and it was vital that we batted them out. A streaky single gave me the strike back and I kept it for two overs – taking twos and a single off the last ball.

The fifty came up at last – 24 of them mine. The runs were just beginning to flow nicely when disaster struck again. I drove a full toss from the spinner along the ground straight back down the pitch. The bowler dived to stop it but missed and I called for a run. Jacky must have been looking over his shoulder at the ball as he ran because he careered straight into the spinner who was still lying on the ground. He fell awkwardly. I stopped running and yelled to Jacky, "Get back!" He tried his best but his leg gave way as he stood up and, with a cry of pain, he fell again. I watched helplessly as the ball came in from the fielder. Jacky was desperately trying to crawl towards the crease when he was run out.

The umpire and I helped him to his feet and he limped off between us. I knew he was really hurt because Jacky doesn't make a fuss about anything. He seemed to have injured his right arm, too, and he held it stiffly across his body as he stumbled along. Then he had another sneezing fit. You couldn't help but feel sorry for him.

I walked back out to the middle with Marty, discussing the best way to get out of the hole we were in. Mart hasn't had a lot of luck with the bat lately and he struggled to give me the strike. With two overs to go, he at last got one in the middle but it flew hard and low towards extra cover. The fielder dived forward and came up appealing with the ball clutched in his hands. I was certain that it had bounced in front of him and, from his reaction, so was Marty. The umpires consulted and after a long wait Marty was given out. He walked off very slowly.

Ohbert ambled out to the middle as if he was setting out to catch butterflies. He forgot to take guard, settled in the crease in his strange crouching stance and looked at the spinner. "Oh but . . . bowl," he grinned.

The ball was just outside the off-stump and Ohbert prodded at it and managed to knee it on to his bat and past the keeper. "Run!" I shouted. I got my bat down as a wild and ridiculously fast throw came in. The keeper couldn't get near it and it flashed through and went for four overthrows – five to Ohbert.

The next ball was short and I pulled it for four. Then I pushed a two into the covers and flicked a single down the leg side. That left Ohbert with one ball of the over to face. It turned out to be two. First he was clean bowled by a no ball – the bowler had stepped on the return crease. Then he played his copybook forward defensive to a long hop and missed by miles. The keeper was so surprised by the shot that he let it through for a bye. 14 runs had come off the over since the fall of Marty's wicket from the first ball. The Thimbledowns were furious and I allowed myself a quiet smile at Great Scott as he changed ends.

Ohbert squared up for the last over of the innings. A great cheer from the boundary greeted the famous "ohfensive" stroke – Ohbert's only other shot. It's practically impossible to describe – a sort of wild swing on one leg with a weird kind of punching action at the end. It was the punch that connected. The ball hit his gloves and cleared the keeper and we ran two. This all came as only a slight surprise to me because although I'd told Ohbert to stop the ball with his pads and run a single, I never really expected him to do what I said.

But next ball, as if suffering from delayed action, he followed my instructions. He rushed down the track and padded the ball away with an exaggerated bend of the knee like a curtsey. The shout for lbw was plain silly since he was miles away from his stumps and we ran a leg-bye. Now I was back on strike again. I squirted a yorker down to fine-leg for two and then top-edged a hook, but it fell safely and we ran three. I wanted to stop at two but Ohbert ignored my shout and ran, to the delight of the Glory Gardens supporters and everyone else who was watching except those supporting Thimbledown.

Ohbert had two to face. He missed the first completely – he even had his bat facing the wrong way – and the ball lobbed over the middle stump. Last ball. "Whatever happens," I told him, "run."

Ohbert went on the "ohfensive" again to an attempted yorker. His eyes were closed but somehow he caught it on the full with the middle of an angled bat. The ball went like a rocket just backward of square. The force of hitting it nearly knocked Ohbert off his feet. The cover-point fielder stopped the ball just short of the boundary but we ran two and I managed to stop

Ohbert going for a third and running himself out. We finished with 81 and, amazing, unbelievable though it was, Ohbert and I had put on 23 unbeaten for the last wicket – it was the highest stand of the innings.

Ohbert was 9 not out and I had 44. But it was Ohbert who got the ovation as we walked in. Frankie and Mack lifted him up on their shoulders and Ohbert sat there blinking and grinning foolishly. The Thimbledown players hardly bothered to clap us off. They immediately went into a huddle with their trainer who didn't look very pleased with their performance.

We might still lose the match, I thought – but at least we now had a fighting chance and Marty and Co. had something to bowl at.

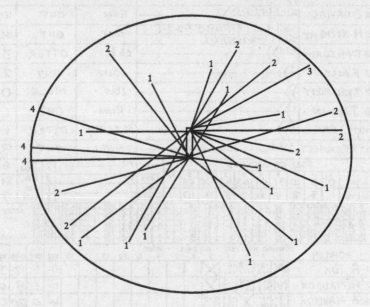

This was Jo's "batogram" of my innings of 44. It shows I play a lot of my shots on the leg side.

Over-s going for a duel and then another three out. We finished with 41 and, amazingly, the double-bounce ball was a 'no' six' and I had put ... on. And, for the 1st wicket ... it was caught by ... ...

Either way, the over and ... had ... ... back, the Chin It was ...

HOME TEAM	GLORY GARDENS	V	THIMBLEDOWN	AWAY TEAM	AT EDG.BASTON	DATE SEPTEMBER 10TH

INNINGS OF GLORY GARDENS .... TOSS WON BY G.G. WEATHER SUNNY

BATSMAN	RUNS SCORED	HOW OUT	BOWLER	SCORE
1 A. NAZAR	≫ — — —	lbw	FOX	0
2 C. SEBASTIEN	2·1·2 ≫ — — —	ST SCOTT	FOX	5
3 C. DA COSTA	≫ — — —	bowled	FOX	0
4 E. DAVIES	2·1·1·1·1·1·2·1 ≫	RUN	OUT	10
5 H. KNIGHT	1·4·1·2·1·1·1·2·1·4·1·2·1·2·2·1 / 2·1·1·1·4·2·1(39)·2·3	NOT	OUT	44
6 T. McCURDY	1·1·1 ≫	c & b	OTTER	3
7 F. ALLEN	2 ≫ — — —	RUN	OUT	2
8 T. VELLACOTT	≫ — — —	lbw	MOLE	0
9 J. GUNN	1 ≫	RUN	OUT	1
10 M. LEAR	1 ≫	CT BARRY	OTTER	1
11 P. BENNETT	5·2·2·	NOT	OUT	9

FALL OF WICKETS											BYES	1·1 — — — — —	2	TOTAL EXTRAS	6
SCORE	1 0	2 0	3 10	4 31	5 41	6 43	7 43	8 55	9 58	10	LBYES 1·1	2	TOTAL	81
BAT NO	1	3	2	4	6	7	8	9	10		WIDES 1	1	FOR	9
											NO BALLS 1	1	WKTS	

SCORE AT A GLANCE

BOWLER	BOWLING ANALYSIS · NO BALL ▲ WIDE													OVS	MDS	RUNS	WKT
	1	2	3	4	5	6	7	8	9	10	11	12	13				
1 B. FOX	WW	·2· 1·2	··2 W··	4· 1··	✕									4	1	12	3
2 W. MADDOX	M	··1 ···	+·11 ···	··2 1··	✕									4	1	9	0
3 A. MADDOX	·1· ·11	·1· 14·	✕	··1 ··1	2·2 2·3									4	0	20	0
4 T. MOLE	2·· 1·2	1·1 1··	W·1 ···	2·1 2·1	✕									4	1	13	1
5 R. OTTER	·1· ·W2	··1 ··1	·12 ·1·	W5· ··	✕									4	0	23	2
6																	
7																	
8																	
9																	

Chapter Eleven

F rankie sang.

> *"The greatest innings you've ever seen*
> *Was it Brian Lara or Azharuddin?*
> *No, we all agree the number one*
> *Was Ohbert's nine at Edgbaston."*

"It was the innings of the tournament, Ohbert. When do you start giving the master classes?" said Azzie, slapping a delighted Ohbert on the back.

"Technically breathtaking," said Cal.

"Outrageous," said Tylan.

Not for the first time in the history of Glory Gardens Ohbert was the unlikely hero of the hour and he was carried shoulder high and squawking the length of the Edgbaston pitch.

The Thimbledowners weren't looking quite so confident now and their trainer was giving them hell. "You let it slip, Gareth," he barked at the Great Scott. "Lost your concentration . . . What did I tell you . . . Never mind – not a big score . . . Just pick them off . . . Fast outfield – plenty of runs." And so he went on in his harsh, aggressive voice, until even I began to feel quite sorry for the Thimbledown players.

But Glory Gardens had its own problems and the biggest of them was Jacky. His wrist was quite badly swollen and he was still limping. "Can you bowl?" I asked him with more hope than expectation.

"Of course," he said picking up a cricket ball and sneezing. But after lobbing a couple of slow ones in my direction he tried coming off his full run and pulled up in agony after half a dozen strides. "It's my knee," he winced. "It just keeps giving way." He was almost in tears as he realised that he wasn't going to be able to bowl.

"Better get some ice on it, kiddo," said Kiddo. "Then maybe we'll get the Warwickshire physio to take a look at it."

I told Matthew he was sub and we took the field. I gave the first over to Erica and Marty warmed up ready to come on at the other end. Great Scott strode confidently out to the middle and faced the first ball. It struck him on the pad and immediately an enormous appeal echoed round the ground.

"You're joking," Gareth turned on Frankie who'd led the shout.

Frankie roared with laughter. "We thought you might like to know what it feels like," he said.

"What do you mean?" stammered the batsman.

"To hear an lbw appeal when the ball's missing leg stump by a foot."

The Scott mumbled something and walked down the wicket to prod at the pitch. Frankie looked at Cal and they both doubled up with laughter again.

Marty's first over was a peach. He really steamed in and gave it everything. Twice the batsman played and missed, then an edge dropped just short of Azzie in the slips and another went for two runs. Finally, with the last ball of the over, he bowled a full toss and the other opener hit it tamely back for an easy return catch.

"Worst ball of the over gets the wicket," said Azzie.

"Look in the book," said Marty over his shoulder as he marched off to his fielding position at long-leg. "It says, caught and bowled Lear. You won't find anything about a lucky full toss."

The second ball of Erica's next over was on a fullish length outside off-stump. Gareth Scott swished at it and there was an

88

audible snick. Frankie took the ball cleanly in both hands. "Howzthat?" he bellowed.

Perhaps it had only been a very slight nick and perhaps the wind was blowing in the wrong direction and maybe the umpire was deaf. Anyway, he stared back down the pitch at Frankie and said, "Not out."

"Not out?" cried Frankie in disbelief. He walked up to Gareth, "You heard it, didn't you? Of course you did, you hit it."

"Another silly appeal," said the Thimbledown captain.

"You mean you didn't hit it?"

"The umpire said, not out – who am I to argue?"

"If you were a sportsman you'd walk."

"Dream on," said Gareth.

Frankie was so wound up he fumbled the next delivery and it went for two byes.

The incident seemed to make everyone more determined. Marty bowled even faster. He beat the bat again and again. Frankie was having a tough time behind the stumps and he gave away more byes with a sloppy piece of keeping. But it didn't seem to worry him; he applauded every ball from Marty and Erica and told both batsmen more than once that he'd never seen anyone as lucky as them in his life.

Then Marty got one to climb off a length and the No. 3 could only fend the ball away with his gloves. Azzie held on to a good slip catch, plucking the ball out of the air as it went past his left ear. And when Marty clean bowled the next man in with an outswinger we were well on top.

At 10 for three the new batsman decided to try and hit Thimbledown out of trouble. His name was Roger Otter; he was the big, broad-shouldered boy whom Ohbert had hit for five runs. Now it was his turn to do some slogging. After top-edging Marty for four he managed to swing a straight ball from Erica over the square-leg boundary. Then Frankie dropped him – a straightforward catch off an edge from a quick one from Marty. Frankie appealed as the ball hit his gloves and I think he was trying to throw it up in the air in triumph when it squeezed out

Marty bowls the perfect outswinger which pitches on middle and hits off-stump. His approach is close to the stumps It ensures that he delivers the ball from sideways-on. At the moment of delivery the wrist locks and the bowler guides the ball with the two top fingers, keeping the seam upright. The right arm follows through across the body and finishes going

of his gloves and fell to the deck.

"You're supposed to catch it first, you idiot," said Marty.

"I did," protested Frankie. "That was a good catch. You don't have to hold on to them for ever you know." But the umpire wasn't the slightest bit convinced.

With a few lucky edges and a couple of nice drives from Great Scott the score raced up to 33 for three. Marty began his last over. The first ball was dug in short to the Thimbledown captain and he went back to hook it. He misread the pace badly and it hit the splice of the bat and went straight up in the air. Frankie had to run round the stumps to take the catch. Gareth stood his ground, precisely on the spot where the ball was about to land. That didn't stop Frankie. He lunged forward as if the batsman wasn't there. The Scott bounced off his stomach and went sprawling on his back. Frankie didn't take his eyes off the ball for a second and, with a dull thud, it landed safely in his gloves.

"HOWZTHAT!" he roared. He looked around for Gareth. "Where's he gone?" Then he saw Gareth struggling to get up and pulled him to his feet. "Great Scott, I think you're out . . . again," he said. Gareth skulked off.

The new batsman fenced unconvincingly at Marty's first ball and swung the next one away in the air to mid-on where Ohbert made an easy catch look impossible. If he'd stood still it would have hit him but he ran about and finished up diving from well out of range. They took a single and Roger Otter squared up to Marty again. Marty beat him completely with a yorker that screamed past his leg stump. Then an enormous heave off the back foot found the middle of the bat and the ball shot like a bullet over mid-wicket for four. Next ball he went for another wild swing and edged to Frankie who took the catch as if he'd never dropped one in his life. He didn't try to throw it up in the air this time, I noticed.

That brought Marty's spell to an end. With five for 12 he'd simply torn the heart out of Thimbledown. It had been the fieriest short spell I could remember seeing him bowl and I only wished he could have carried on and finished them off. But as Marty slouched off to his fielding position at long-leg, it was now up to the rest of us to complete the job he'd started. Cal took over from Erica, who had been as steady as ever, and I replaced Marty.

Things went from bad to worse for Thimbledown. Cal failed to pick up a ball driven hard back at him along the ground. He recovered quickly and chased after it. The striker called for a run but was sent back. He turned a fraction too late and must have been utterly amazed when he saw Cal's low hard throw demolish his stumps. Then it was my turn; my slower ball completely deceived the new batsman and he holed out to Erica at extra-cover for a duck.

Cal virtually wrapped it up when he bowled their No. 7 next over and then lured the new batter down the wicket to give

Frankie an easy stumping. The last pair hung around for a bit without scoring too many runs but finally with a full six overs to go I got my second wicket and Azzie his second slip catch. We'd bowled them out for 48.

"If they're the best team in the competition, what are we?" said Tylan.

"You can thank Marty for that victory," said Cal. "I thought he bowled out of his skin."

Marty blushed a little and looked quite pleased. Then he remembered he was Marty. "It won't make any difference. If Langbottom beat Thimbledown we still go out of the competition."

"He's right," said Frankie. "We'd better cheer for the Thimbledowners. They need a bit of support to build up their confidence after that thrashing."

Most of the Thimbledown team had mysteriously vanished at the end of the game. I looked for Gareth Scott to shake hands with him – but he'd disappeared, too.

"Great Scott, where've they all gone?" said Frankie.

Probably getting out of the way of their trainer, I thought.

HOME TEAM	GLORY GARDENS	V	THIMBLEDOWN	AWAY TEAM	AT EDGBASTON DATE SEPTEMBER 10

INNINGS OF THIMBLEDOWN .... TOSS WON BY G.G. WEATHER SUNNY

BATSMAN	RUNS SCORED	HOW OUT	BOWLER	SCORE
1 G. SCOTT	1·2·2·1·1·2·1 >> - - · · · · ·	ct ALLEN	LEAR	10
2 B. FOX	1·2 >> · · · · · · · --- -----	c & b	LEAR	3
3 T. MOLE	>> · --- -- ------ -	ct NAZAR	LEAR	0
4 J. DENNIS	>> --- - · ···-- -	bowled	LEAR	0
5 R. OTTER	4·4·3·4 >> -- ------ ----	ct ALLEN	LEAR	15
6 B. BARRY	1·1 >> ---- -- · · --	RUN	OUT	2
7 T. YOUNG	1·1 >> -- ----- · -··	bowled	SEBASTIEN	2
8 H. HUSBAND	>> - ------- --- - ---···	ct DAVIES	KNIGHT	0
9 W. MADDOX	1·2 · · · ------- ·	NOT	OUT	3
10 J. FORD	>> ···	st ALLEN	SEBASTIEN	0
11 A. MADDOX	2·2 >> --	ct NAZAR	KNIGHT	4

FALL OF WICKETS											BYES	2·2·2· --- ---	6	TOTAL EXTRAS	9
SCORE	4	10	10	33	38	40	41	41	41	48	L BYES	2·1	3	TOTAL FOR	48
BAT NO	2	3	4	1	5	6	8	7	10	11	WIDES				
											NO BALLS			WKTS	10

SCORE AT A GLANCE

BOWLER	BOWLING ANALYSIS · NO BALL + WIDE													OVS	MDS	RUNS	WKT
	1	2	3	4	5	6	7	8	9	10	11	12	13				
1 E. DAVIES	··· !	··· ·	·2 !	3·2	X									4	0	17	0
	1·· 1	2···	··4	··1													
2 M. LEAR	···	·W·	·W·!	·N·!	X									4	0	12	5
	2·W	·W4·	··· ·	·4·W													
3 C. SEBASTIEN	·· !	·W·	·2·											3	0	6	2
	1··	W·2															
4 H. KNIGHT	·!·	··· ·	··2											3	0	4	2
	W·!	1···	··W														
5																	
6																	
7																	
8																	
9																	

Chapter Twelve

"It's a funny old game, kiddoes," mused Kiddo, the way he often does.

"Don't ask him why," whispered Frankie. "Or we'll get one of his stories."

But there's no stopping Kiddo when he gets that look in his eyes. "Did I ever tell you about the first limited-overs game I played in?"

"I'm sure you must have, Mr Johnstone," Frankie said firmly.

Kiddo took no notice, he was already in full swing and wouldn't be put off by Frankie or anyone. "We batted first," he began. "There were eight lbws – half of them decidedly dodgy, I remember – a bit like your game. We were all out for 47. And then guess what happened?"

"It was rained off?" ventured Tylan.

"No, kiddo. They scored ten runs off the first over from our quickie and we switched tack and brought on the spinners. The game turned round completely and, would you believe it, we bowled them out for 40."

"Knock me down with a googly," said Frankie.

"So you see, kiddoes. Anything can happen on a cricket field. Just when you think you're finished, something can come along which turns round the entire game."

"Like lunch," said Frankie. "And it's time we had ours."

"You're not having any," said Jo.

"Don't start that again. I'm starving!"

"She means you're not having lunch with us," said Cal. "We

ordered you a special packed lunch from the restaurant. It's calorie-controlled." He handed Frankie a small paper carrier bag.

"What's this?" asked Frankie. One by one he took out the contents of the bag. "An apple. A pear. A sandwich . . ."

"Cucumber on rye bread, I think," said Cal.

"A carton of blackberry yoghurt. And what's this?"

"Carrot cake."

"I'm not eating this. Oh I get it . . . it's a joke. Ha ha . . . all right let's go and have some proper food."

"'Fraid not, fatman. You're not booked in," Cal grinned. "Now we don't want to be late for our burgers and chips, so we'll leave you to your picnic."

"Bon appetit," said Tylan slapping Frankie on the back. Frankie groaned and slumped on to the bench with his calorie-controlled lunch. Gatting came over to sniff it but even he didn't look very impressed.

Lunch was in the indoor school across the car park. The results of all the morning's games were up on the notice board when we went in.

LEAGUE A

Edmondleigh lost to Cherrystanton by 8 wickets
Elphinstone Forest beat Bishops Ardley by 21 runs
Bishops Ardley lost to Edmondleigh by 7 wickets
Cherrystanton beat Elphinstone Forest by 18 runs

LEAGUE B

Glory Gardens lost to Langbottom by 2 runs
Thimbledown lost to Glory Gardens by 33 runs

"Looks like Cherrystanton for the final," said Cal.

"They're one of the favourites," said Jo.

"Like Thimbledown were," said Tylan. "Before Glory Gardens sorted them."

Everyone at lunch couldn't stop talking about the missing

Cragg Moor team.

"Perhaps they've disappeared down a ravine and all perished," said Marty.

"Or been hijacked and held to ransom," suggested Tylan.

"If you don't stop behaving like children, I'm going to eat my lunch somewhere else," said Jo. "Actually their coach broke down."

"How do you know?"

"I asked one of the organisers. He said they had engine trouble."

"Well I don't think it's fair," said an Edmondleigh player. "We've got to play three games in our league and you're only playing two."

"It's not our fault if Cragg Moor's bus has packed up," said Matthew suddenly. Matthew doesn't say much and when he does he goes very red in the cheeks.

"Don't worry, Matt," said Cal. "They're a bit upset because Cherrystanton massacred them and because they didn't sleep too well last night."

The Edmondleigh player went back to eating his lunch in silence.

After the break there was no sign of Frankie or his lunch. Gatting had disappeared, too, and Kiddo went off to look for him. Jacky set off for a session with the physiotherapist – his leg was still hurting him and he was limping badly. He told me he was feeling a lot better but that was because he wanted to play. His knee was badly swollen and going purple and it was my guess that he was out of the tournament. The rest of us hung around waiting for the next game to start.

Jacky wasn't the only Glory Gardens player on the injury list. Clive was getting one of his headaches. Clive doesn't like to leave you in any doubt when he's sick. He always makes a big drama out of the slightest knock or illness – all you hear is how much he is suffering. So now this was the worst headache he'd ever had in his life. It was quite impossible to tell whether he was faking it or really getting one of his migraines.

Fortunately he went off to lie down so we didn't have to listen to any more of his complaints. The game between Langbottom and Thimbledown was about to begin and if Langbottom won we were out of the finals.

"We'll still be in the play-off for third and fourth place," said Azzie.

"We will if Langbottom wins," said Jo.

"And if they lose?"

"Then anything can happen. We could be first, second or third."

"So what are the rules if we all get the same points?" asked Erica.

By now Jo had done her homework. "It's worked out on the total number of runs scored in the league games."

"How many have we got?" asked Azzie.

"After two games our total's 172. So if Langbottom scores 80 or Thimbledown 125, then we're in trouble."

"There's no way Thimbledown will knock 125," said Mack.

"It's not very likely they'll win either," said Marty gloomily.

Cal threw a pad at him. "It's so good having you around, Marty – cheering us up all the time. Can't you ever look on the bright side?"

"I can't stand being disappointed," said Marty.

"That's no reason to be miserable."

"Yes, it is," said Marty. "If I'm right, then I'm ready for the bad news. And if I'm wrong I get a nice surprise."

"I still think it's a funny way to look at things," said Cal.

Langbottom batted and after a couple of overs Cal and I decided to go and watch a bit of the Cherrystanton game over on the practice ground. If we were to get to the final it would be useful to know something about the opposition. We thought we might find Frankie and Gatting there, too.

"Who's in the team for the next game – if there is one?" asked Cal, when we were out of earshot of the rest.

"I'm not sure yet," I said. "If Jacky can't bowl I'd like to play

Kris as an extra bowler."

"And who are you going to drop this time? Ohbert? Or Mack maybe?" said Cal.

"I don't want to drop either of them, especially Mack – he's too good a fielder, even though he hasn't been batting too well lately. And how can I leave Ohbert out after the Thimbledown game?"

Cal laughed. "Sometimes I can't believe Glory Gardens has had all this success with Ohbert playing for us."

"Maybe he brings us luck."

"Maybe he's so awful he confuses the opposition," said Cal. "Anyway, I agree with you. I don't think we should drop him if we get through. Perhaps Clive will be too ill to play."

That wasn't an appealing thought either. "Let's worry about who's playing when we know we've got a game," I said.

"It's a terrible responsibility being captain," said Cal sarcastically.

"Maybe it's time you found out again."

"About what?"

"About the strain and the responsibility. If we make it all the way to the final, how would you like to be captain?"

"Why should I? We've already got a captain."

"And don't worry, I'm not resigning," I said. "But I've been talking to Azzie and Marty. We think you did a great job in the first game when we were playing for the Colts. And if you hadn't won we wouldn't be here. So how about it?"

"What if I say yes and we lose?"

"If you can't stand the heat, you'd better forget it."

"In that case, I accept," said Cal. "If it's okay with the rest."

"That's a relief. Then you can pick the team with Jo and Marty," I said.

Chapter Thirteen

W e didn't have to watch Cherrystanton for long to realise they were special. Even if we made it to the final we were going to have to play out of our skins to have a chance of beating them.

Their two openers were in the Azzie class – fluent, almost carefree stroke-makers but with a good, tight defence to match. They'd put on 20 so easily that it was a surprise when one of them was out, caught on the boundary. Their No. 3 came in. He was a left-hander and he simply tore the Bishops Ardley bowling apart. But it was their running between the wickets which really impressed me. You could see they'd been coached hard to play limited-overs cricket – and they didn't miss a trick.

"Look at that," gasped Cal. "Matthew would never have thought of taking a run there. But there was no risk at all."

"If we play them we just can't leave out Mack," I said. "Look at the pressure they're putting on the cover fielders."

The score was rattling along. After 10 overs Cherrystanton had 59 on the board.

"I think I've seen enough," said Cal. "Let's come back later and see them bowl." At that moment an enormous six cleared the square-leg boundary and bounced into the crowd.

"Fine shot, Jeremy," shouted a large red-faced man with a growly voice who was sitting just behind us – probably Jeremy's dad, we thought. "Now don't go wild, old son. Keep the concentration flowing."

Jeremy was the left-hander. He's the sort of player who, as

Kiddo would say, knows how to put himself about. His shouts of "Wait" and "Come on" were loud enough to wake the dead. He even called "Wait" when he let the ball go through to the Bishops' keeper.

"If he does that to Frankie he'll get an earful," I said.

"And a load of byes, too," said Cal. "If only Frankie could learn to concentrate he'd be a good keeper."

"Dream on," I said. "And where do you think our keeper's gone?"

"Probably off in search of a second lunch. He'll turn up, fatter than ever, you'll see."

When we got back to the league B game on the main pitch the Langbottom innings was just coming to its close. With two balls to go they were on 77 for six.

"They started well but lost four quick wickets," Azzie told us.

We watched the next delivery beat the bat and everything else and go through to the keeper. The bowler buried his head in his hands and nearly wept with frustration. His last ball was a low full toss and it was dispatched on the leg side for two. Final score: 79 for six. Now it was Thimbledown's chance to put us in the final. At least that's how we saw it.

"Come on, Scotty," shouted Tylan as the Thimbledown captain went out to bat. "Let's see a proper innings from you this time. We're counting on you." Gareth Scott scowled at him and Tylan laughed. "No sense of humour, that's his trouble," he said.

There was still no sign of Frankie. "I bet it's his diet," said Marty. "He could be lying somewhere too weak to move."

"Or perhaps he's just faded away to nothing," said Cal.

"The incredible shrinking Frankie," said Tylan.

"Ohbert's gone, too," said Azzie. "He must have just wandered off while we were watching the cricket."

"It's getting like an Agatha Christie story," said Cal. "I wonder how many of us will be left by nightfall."

"The Team that Vanished," said Tylan in a spooky voice.

The Thimbledown innings started shakily with the loss of two early wickets but Gareth Scott started to pull things back and slowly they edged ahead of the required run rate. Jo kept us posted at the end of every over.

As the overs ran out it got more and more tense. Another wicket fell. Marty was chewing his fingernails and even Cal was pacing about.

"I can't stand this, it's worse than watching Ohbert batting," said Tylan. "I think I'll go and look for Frankie."

"Don't get lost," said Cal. "It looks as if we're going to need your bowling." He pointed in the direction of the pavilion from where Jacky was limping slowly towards us. Even before he spoke we knew he was out of the competition.

"He won't let me play," he said glumly. "That rotten physio says I need to have my ligament checked out and I can't run until I see a doctor."

"How's the wrist?" asked Cal.

"Oh that's all right," sighed Jacky. "Just bruised."

"So that means we're down to twelve; eleven if Clive can't play," calculated Erica.

"Nine if Frankie and Ohbert don't show up," said Marty.

"Is Clive still asleep?" I asked.

"Yes, snoring away with a towel over his head," said Azzie. "You can hear him from here if you listen."

Thimbledown had now edged well ahead. The Great Scott was in the 40s and they needed only 5 to win with nearly three overs to go. A cover drive for four brought the scores level and the very next ball Gareth went back and hooked. The ball raced across the boundary to give him his 50. In the end it was an easy victory. But what did we care – we just wanted to know what it meant for us.

"Are we in the final?" Azzie demanded, standing impatiently over Jo, who was calculating the results.

"I don't believe it," said Jo.

"What?"

"I know. We've lost," said Marty.

"Just look at this," said Jo.

	Played	Won	Lost	Points	Total Runs
Glory Gardens	2	1	1	4	172
Langbottom	2	1	1	4	172
Thimbledown	2	1	1	4	129

"We've drawn . . . or is it tied?" cried Azzie. "We've got the same run total as Langbottom."

"What does that mean?" I asked Jo.

"It means this," said Jo, reading carefully from her copy of the rules of the competition. *"If two or more teams have the same points total and runs total, the winner will be decided by a stumps competition. Each team shall select six bowlers to bowl one ball at the stumps from the full length of the pitch. The team scoring the most hits will be declared the winner. If at the end of the first round the scores are level, then the players will continue to bowl until one team is ahead."*

"So we need six bowlers," said Erica.

"And every one has got to hit the stumps," said Azzie like a typical batsman.

I called out the names: "Marty, Erica, Cal, Tylan," – Ty had just returned without sighting Frankie – "me and . . ." I was about to say Kris when Jacky interrupted.

"I can bowl. I don't have to run up. Having a bad leg won't make any difference, I promise."

"As long as you don't sneeze while I'm bowling," said Tylan.

What could I say? Jacky had had enough disappointments for one day and he was probably right. His experience would be useful if we came under pressure. "Okay," I said. "We'd better go and have a practice."

Over to our right an almighty row had broken out. The Thimbledown supporters and players had surrounded one of the officials and they were getting very excited indeed. We moved closer to try and hear what was going on.

"Those are the rules – I can't do anything about it," said the official.

"It's not fair," shouted the blond Thimbledown trainer, his

face white with rage and his arms waving about like a windmill.

"Whose rules are they anyway?" demanded one of the parents. "I want to know who is responsible for such stupid rules. We've come a long way for this tournament, you know and really . . ."

"But I can't see what's wrong with them," stammered the poor official. All the Thimbledown parents and supporters were squeezing round him. The players were standing to one side, looking confused.

"It's obvious, man," continued the bossy parent. "They penalise the team batting second. How are you to know Thimbledown wouldn't have gone on to score 150 or even 200?"

"Seems unlikely to me," said the official, trying unsuccessfully to stop things getting out of control.

"That's what they said to Christopher Columbus," said the parent. "Now I think you should admit the rules are wrong and let all three teams go into the stumps competition."

"Well I'm afraid I can't, and that's that," said the official rather crossly.

"In that case I shall write to Lords about it," said the trainer.

"Outrageous," said Tylan. "If only Frankie could see this."

"I knew they were bad losers the moment I saw them," said Jo.

"Well you can't blame the team. They aren't the ones who are complaining," said Azzie.

"Just imagine having parents like that though," said Cal. "I'd die of shame."

"We forced ourselves away from the blazing row and the six of us practised bowling at a single wicket for ten minutes before we were called over to start the competition.

I won the toss and we bowled first. We had already decided on a bowling order and Marty led the way. He came in off a short run and seemed somehow to try too hard to go for accuracy. He got in a real tangle and the ball went way down the leg side. Langbottom went next and their captain, Asad Butt, opened the score by hitting off-stump.

My turn now. I knew we needed to bounce back immediately.

103

Bowling straight takes lots and lots of practice but one useful tip is to take aim like this. Look down the pitch at your target from behind the "aiming" arm and shoulder and as your hand comes through watch it go through the target.

As I released the ball I knew it was spot on target; a moment later the middle stump was lying back.

"Great ball, Hooker," shouted Azzie from the stands. But Langbottom hit back straight away to go 2–1 up. Then Cal missed by a whisker. And so did the next Langbottom player – he looked crossly at Jacky who had sneezed just at the moment he released the ball.

With three to go on each side, Erica just managed to clip the off-stump and one bail fell. We were level again. Their third bowler missed and so did Tylan. Then, disaster; the fifth Langbottom player scattered the stumps with a slow full toss. It was 3–2 to them.

Jacky took the ball and stared hard at the far wicket. If he missed we were out of the final. He stepped back about five yards from the crease and again he fixed his eyes on the target. At last he limped in, just three strides, and bowled. At first I thought he'd missed. The ball pitched just outside off-stump but it cut in off the pitch and hammered into the stumps. There was a huge cheer.

"Three all," shouted Cal. And three all it stayed because, as we held our breath, the last Langbottom bowler missed by inches.

So now it was sudden death and Marty to bowl first. "Just pretend you're bowling in a match, Mart," said Cal quietly in Marty's ear.

And Marty did. He steamed in off his full run and a straight yorker blasted away the middle stump. When the Glory Gardens cheers died down, the Langbottom skipper took a deep breath and bowled. I looked away. There was no sound of the ball hitting the stump – only a gasp from the bowler – and then a second's silence and a roar of triumph from the Glory Gardens players.

Without a word I turned and shook hands with Asad Butt. Suddenly I felt really sorry for him. After all, his team had beaten us earlier and they'd gone out in a silly stumps competition which didn't really prove anything. But he couldn't have been more sporting. "Well played," he said. "I hope you win." And then it struck me. Against all the odds Glory Gardens were through. We'd made it through to the final!

Chapter Fourteen

O ur path to the final hadn't been altogether glorious but that didn't stop us celebrating. I don't think any of us had expected to get this far in the competition and I've never seen Glory Gardens so excited. Everyone was talking at once. Even Matthew, who is usually so quiet you forget he's there, was shouting at the top of his voice and Erica, Jo and Kris even sang one of Frankie's Glory Gardens songs.

After a while Kiddo had to tell us to calm down and remember we still had a big game to play. "I'm not saying that you shouldn't be proud of yourselves, kiddoes," he said. "But, if you get carried away, you'll blow it in the big game."

He told us to go and sit down quietly and think how we were going to play the final. "And, if you lose," he added, "you might remember the way those Langbottom lads behaved when they were knocked out."

Unfortunately Thimbledown weren't showing the Langbottom sporting spirit; the big row was still going on in front of the score-board and it was as ever the parents who were causing all the trouble. The poor man they'd been attacking before had now been joined by two other officials in blue blazers and things were getting even nastier. A big woman screamed at the top of her voice. "My husband's a solicitor and you'll be hearing from him." The trainer was shouting and waving his programme and there was a lot of pushing and shoving.

"It's so silly to argue about it," said Jo. "Can't they see it's the same rules for everyone."

"I think there's going to be a punch-up," said Tylan. But before it happened Kiddo waved us away. "It's pathetic," he sighed. "And it's always the same with parents; they get over-involved and then this sort of business happens. They shouldn't be allowed in."

"I don't think my dad would go on like that," said Azzie.

"No, you're right, kiddo." Kiddo smiled. "But then he's a proper Glory Gardens' supporter and he understands about cricket. This rabble hasn't got the first clue. Forget about them – we've got more important business." He turned to me. "Have you picked your team yet, Harry?"

I shook my head. "Ask the skipper," I said, nodding in Cal's direction. For the first time I felt a touch of disappointment about handing the captaincy over to Cal. This was going to be Glory Gardens' biggest game and I really wanted to be in charge. Everyone had supported the idea of Cal being captain in the final – in fact, maybe they'd been a little too keen on the idea. Anyway it was too late to change things now.

I thought Kiddo looked a bit surprised but he didn't say anything. He's good like that – he lets us get on with running the team the way we want to without interfering.

"It shouldn't be too hard to pick a team," said Cal to Kiddo. "Right now we've only got nine players."

Kiddo set off in search of the missing Ohbert, Frankie and Gatting and we went for tea.

———————————— • ————————————

Our opponents in the final were Cherrystanton. No surprise there. They'd bowled Bishops Ardley out for 30 and won by a massive margin of 85 runs.

"It's a pity we didn't get a chance to see them bowl," said Cal. "They must be pretty awesome."

This was how league A finished:

	Played	Won	Lost	Points
Cherrystanton	3	3	0	12
Edmondleigh	3	2	1	8
Elphinstone For.	3	1	2	4
Bishops Ardley	3	0	3	0

After tea there was still no sign of Frankie, Ohbert or Gatting. Kiddo returned empty-handed; he was getting quite anxious because Gatting's usually too lazy to wander off.

Clive was still asleep. With the final due to start in ten minutes, the situation was looking serious. Jo reminded us if we couldn't find eleven players for the final we'd be disqualified.

"I can see why you don't want to be captain," said Cal to me. "This is embarrassing."

"I'll go and wake Clive," said Azzie, "and tell him his team needs him."

Cal was just setting off with the Cherrystanton captain to toss up when I noticed the unmistakable figure of Frankie ambling over towards us; he was wearing his wicket-keeping pads and gloves. "Here comes your keeper," I shouted to Cal who waved a fist in Frankie's direction.

Frankie was grinning from ear to ear and he brushed aside our boos and insults. Just for a moment he looked anxiously at Jo who was standing hands on hips waiting for an explanation; then the grin returned.

"Calm down, you lot. I've only been practising."

"Practising stuffing your face, I bet," said Marty.

"Well, I did have a little snackette," said Frankie. "That's where I met them."

"Who?"

"Didn't I tell you? The Warwickshire team. I've been having a net with Nick and the boys."

"You don't mean Nick Knight . . ."

"You bet," said Frankie. "Of course I gave Keith Piper a few little wicket-keeping tips... and he gave me a couple in return. Wait till I show you."

"I wonder, did you catch the news that we're through to the final," said Erica casually.

"Of course I did. I've been listening to it all on the loudspeakers."

"Then why didn't you come back earlier?"

"I decided to keep you all in suspense – serves you right after the way you've been starving me."

"You're lucky to be picked at all," said Jo. "It's only because Jacky's injured and Ohbert's missing that you're in the team."

Frankie frowned and shook his head. "You're pulling my leg. How could you think of playing without your star wicket-keeper?"

The arrival of Clive cut short Jo's reply. He looked fine after his sleep. His headache had completely gone and he was ready for action, too. At last we had a team – with Ohbert still missing there were just eleven of us:

Matthew Rose	Mack McCurdy
Cal Sebastien (capt.)	Frankie Allen
Azzie Nazar	Kris Johansen
Clive da Costa	Tylan Vellacott
Erica Davies	Marty Lear
Hooker Knight	

Cal returned from the middle and called us all together. "Are you ready for my 'team talk'?" he asked shyly.

"He's not captain, is he?" said Frankie with a snort of laughter.

"I'll talk to you later about your fine for being late, fatman," said Cal. "But first we're going to win this game. Marty will tell you who the favourites are - and it's not us. But, in case Frankie's interested in a bet, my money's on Glory Gardens. I'll tell you why. In a big game we always lift ourselves and rise to the challenge. So, just remember, if we win we're the best team in the country; that's what we're playing for. That means we've got to chase every ball, run every single, hang on to every catch . . ."

Frankie yawned.

"Okay," said Cal. "I've finished. We're fielding by the way."

"Then let's get out there and sort them," said Frankie jumping to his feet.

"What have you been stuffing into yourself, fatman?" Cal asked Frankie as we took the field.

"I had chicken, chips and roast potatoes in the players' canteen," said Frankie. "Best meal I've ever had."

"Chips *and* roast potatoes," sighed Cal.

"Yes, the diet's off – that's official," said Frankie. "And I'm never doing it again."

"Good decision. You've got to look after your well-rounded personality," said Tylan.

Marty marked out his run and bowled a few practice deliveries at me. We all knew that, with Jacky out, a lot rested on Marty's bowling. I was pleased to see he was looking really sharp and fired up. Cal asked me to bowl from the other end.

Marty's first three balls were short outside the off-stump and Frankie took them all cleanly. "It works, see," he said to Azzie and me. "That's just what Keith told me to do. Rise with the ball, head steady, relax."

A keeper should start to rise from the crouching stance as the bowler bowls. Aim to get your hands on the line and height of the ball. Stay relaxed and aim to take the ball with both hands – but don't spread the fingers too wide. Above all don't point your fingers at the ball or you will break them.

An over-pitched ball from Marty was driven for two. Then the opener cut another short one hard into the ground. It flew high to Mack's left and he leapt like a salmon and managed to knock it up in the air. The batsman had already set off for the run; he stopped dead in his tracks and turned. Mack caught the ball with his back to the wicket and in one movement fired at the stumps. With only one stump to aim at it was a miracle throw. The batsman was left a foot short of his crease gasping in amazement as the bails flew high in the air. No other fielder in the side, or probably in the tournament, would have attempted a stunt like that.

Frankie caught one of the bails and threw it over his head. We rushed over to congratulate Mack. "Brilliant, Mack. Brilliant. That'll make them think," enthused Cal.

"Never take liberties with Glory Gardens' fielding," said Frankie.

The retreating batsman still had a shocked look on his face. He simply couldn't believe what had happened to him.

"2 for one – not a bad start," said Cal. "Now let's keep it tight."

Marty finished his over and I came on at the other end. A leg-bye brought me face to face with the new batsman who was none other than Jeremy, their star left-hand bat – he was also the Cherrystanton captain.

"We know he's good," said Cal, "especially off his legs. So what field setting do you want for him?"

Bowling left-arm over to a left-hander, the natural line of my deliveries will cut into his legs. If I got it too straight he'd hammer me away on the leg side. "I'll try and keep them outside off-stump," I said. "Give me five on the off and four on the leg side." This was the field I bowled to.

Only once in the over did I drift in direction and it cost me four runs – the offending ball was smartly dispatched to the boundary past square-leg. It was a good over otherwise, spoilt by one lousy delivery and I wasn't very pleased with myself when I took my place in the gully for Marty's next over.

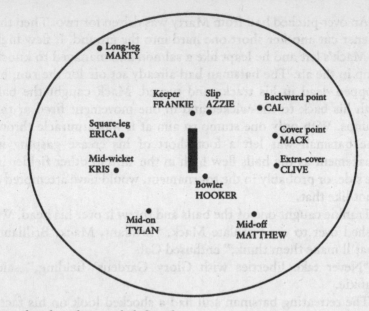

Hooker bowling to left-hander

"Why don't you go round the wicket to him," suggested Azzie. I'd thought of that but decided it was a bit defensive for the opening overs. "I'd never get an lbw going round. Maybe later," I mumbled.

"Look, the supporters have arrived," cried Frankie, pointing to the boundary where Ohbert and Gatting had just joined Kiddo, Jacky and Jo in the lower tier of the pavilion stand. "Welcome back, Ohbert," he shouted.

Ohbert, just for once, wasn't wearing his Walkman and he heard Frankie's cry and waved back; a silly toothy grin spread across his face.

"It's nice to see our mascots again," said Tylan. "I wonder where they've been hiding."

It wasn't long before we found out. The sun was slanting straight into the keeper's eyes from behind the pavilion as Marty bowled and Frankie called for a cap. Ohbert was sent out with it.

"Where on earth have you been, Ohbert?" snapped Marty. "We

112

might have needed you."

"Oh but . . . I've been to the museum," spluttered Ohbert. "It's got some really funny pictures in it."

"Can you remember why you came here today, Ohbert?" said Frankie, who had conveniently forgotten that he'd been missing all afternoon, too.

"But . . . I thought it would be easier for you," said Ohbert.

"What would?"

"Oh but . . . picking the team . . . if I wasn't there. Marty said it was going to be very hard choosing who to drop."

"So you volunteered?" said Azzie.

"Sort of," said Ohbert, trotting back to his seat.

"I've a funny feeling that Ohbert has sacrificed himself for the team," said Erica.

"Strange. That must mean that he knows he's useless," said Frankie.

"It means we'd better win the trophy for him," said Cal. "Let's get on with it."

Chapter Fifteen

My second over went for ten runs and it wasn't even a bad one – apart from the last ball, a full toss. But then Jeremy Pike is a class batsman and he doesn't miss many scoring chances. The full toss was dispatched with no effort at all between cover and extra-cover for four. I stood and watched it bounce over the boundary rope with a feeling of helplessness.

"I'm going to rest you and try Tylan," said Cal. "He may find it a bit more difficult to get the spinners away."

I wasn't pleased. I hadn't bowled badly and I didn't like being taken off after only two overs. However, I could see Cal's point – just. Cherrystanton were going along at five an over and something had to be done now to stop the flow of runs.

Marty's next over was his quickest yet. He hit the opening bat in the chest and then went past his outstretched bat and off-stump with a beauty that swung late. It swung past Frankie, too and went for three byes. Even Jeremy had difficulty handling Marty and he very nearly played an inside edge on to his stumps. The ball again eluded Frankie's despairing dive and went for two runs down to long-leg.

Marty gave the Cherrystanton batsman a long, cold stare as if to say, I don't like batsmen, especially lucky ones.

Tylan opened with a wide down the leg side. "That means he'll bowl well," said Frankie. "He always does when he starts with a wide."

Tylan immediately got the ball to turn and, as long as he kept it on a length, he was treated with great respect by both batsmen.

114

But there's always a loose ball or two in every Tylan over and, sure enough, his long hop got the full treatment, although Erica's diving stop on the mid-wicket boundary prevented it going for four and saved us two runs.

Marty rounded off his four-over spell with a maiden – though Frankie kept the score-board rolling by letting two more byes through his legs. Cherrystanton had now reached 30 off seven overs.

The second ball of Tylan's next over was slightly over-pitched and it must have stopped a bit. Jeremy drove it straight back down the track in the air. It went like a rocket at head height to Tylan and although he got both hands to the catch, it burst through his fingers and hit him smack on the nose. Ty picked up the ball, shied at the stumps, missed – Jeremy probably had his bat in anyway – and Cal dived to stop the overthrows.

"Hard luck, Ty . . ." I began. Then I noticed the blood pouring from his nose. Both umpires rushed up to help him and one of them gave him a handkerchief. Tylan eventually walked off with the handkerchief clasped to his bloody nose. I knew exactly how he felt – when you drop a catch like that off your own bowling it's bad enough, but getting injured too is the final straw.

Cal had a word with one of the umpires and signalled for Ohbert to come on as substitute. Ohbert, of course, ignored him and it wasn't until the whole team was waving and shouting at him that he eventually worked out what we wanted.

"Super-sub's wide awake as usual!" said Frankie grinning at Ohbert who shuffled on to the field in his bright green and orange pullover. Cal told him to take it off and eventually Ohbert settled down somewhere near mid-on.

Cal marked out his run – he was going to bowl the last four balls of Tylan's over. He set himself a strong leg-side field for the right-hander and bowled a middle-and-leg line. It worked reasonably well but the trouble came when Cal had to adjust his direction for the left-hander. His first ball to Jeremy gave him too much width outside the off-stump and it was cracked away for four to extra-cover's left.

Erica replaced Marty and did her normal, good containing job. There are no tricks or frills to Erica's bowling – she just bowls straight with the simple idea: if you miss I hit. There are not many batters prepared to take liberties with that sort of bowling.

At the other end Cal was having a lot more difficulty bowling wicket to wicket and his next over went for seven runs. At the half way stage Cherrystanton had scored 47 – but the real worry was that they had lost only one wicket.

The 50 was notched up in the next over when Ohbert let a ball run between his legs to give away a single. But, if we groaned at that, we were soon to be cheering.

Cal had just been pulled for two runs and I was beginning to think it was time to interfere and tell him to drop the field back. If we carried on attacking like this Cherrystanton would just pick off the boundaries at will. Cal's next ball was again shortish and the right-hander went for another cross-batted shot on the leg side. Somehow he got underneath it and top-edged the ball high in the air. It went up a long way but it was a straight catch to mid-on – except mid-on was Ohbert.

Cal spotted the problem immediately and ran for the catch shouting, "Mine, Mine, Ohbert. Leave it!" Ohbert was running round in circles, looking up at the ball and making squeaking noises. Then suddenly he said in a very loud voice, "It's mine, Cal." Cal stopped.

The two batsmen had started to run but now their eyes were fixed firmly on Ohbert. Who could ignore him as he flapped and circled under the descending ball? There was a clatter of bats and pads as the batsmen ran straight into each other. At exactly the same moment the ball went past Ohbert's outstretched hands, past his nose and landed in front of him. As it hit the ground Ohbert launched a kick at it, why I'll never know, but – and this is the amazing bit – he kicked it straight into the hands of Cal who was standing about five yards away.

Cal looked at the ball, turned, saw the batsmen struggling to their feet in the middle of the pitch and threw – not at the bowler's stumps but to Frankie. Frankie caught it over the stumps and flicked off the bails. Instead of catching the opening bat Ohbert had run out Jeremy. No-one could believe it, least of all Jeremy. He glared at Ohbert and Ohbert grinned back.

"He always uses his feet," said Frankie. "Either that or he heads it across to me and I back-heel it on to the stumps. Easy."

Jeremy looked at the stumps again, blinked and shook his head. He started to say something but nothing came out. In the end he just walked off, still shaking his head. The score-board said 54 for two. Two balls later it was 54 for three as Cal took a simple caught and bowled off the new batsman. Suddenly – and thanks to Ohbert – we were back in the match.

Tylan returned to the field. His nose was red but the bleeding had stopped. We applauded Ohbert as he went off and he got a big cheer from all the neutrals in the crowd, too. But I don't think the Cherrystanton supporters were quite so impressed with his brief contribution.

Cal continued his defensive line to the two right-handers. The new batsman was a hitter; by that I don't mean a slogger – he played pretty straight but with a lot of right hand. After a couple of expansive drives which went straight to the field, he belted Cal over the top for four. Then the opener, who had played so well, lifted a leg flick to Mack at square-leg. He had to dive forward to take the catch but he grabbed it in both hands. 69 for four was the score with just five overs and two balls remaining.

Erica finished her spell and Cal ran in to bowl another over but the umpire stopped him. "You've already bowled four overs, laddie," he said.

"No I haven't," protested Cal. "The first one was Tylan's . . . eh, I mean, Vellacott's. I just finished it for him." The umpires conferred and in spite of Cal's protest they decided he would have to change bowlers.

"Quite right," said Clive. "Give someone else a chance – like me."

But Cal threw the ball to Tylan again. I wasn't sure about that – Tylan's an attacking bowler and this wasn't the time to go on the attack. Anyway I wanted to bowl. I wasn't too pleased with Cal for taking me off after two overs and now it didn't look as if he was going to let me bowl again.

Tylan seemed to be still suffering from his nose injury. He bowled a long hop which was clattered for four and followed that with two wides. The score was mounting fast and we really needed a couple of tight overs to steady things down. Instead ten runs came off the over and I only just stopped myself going over to Cal to demand what was going on. Then he called up Kris to bowl at the other end.

I'm not saying Kris isn't a good bowler – she can be nearly as quick as Marty – but at a moment like this we needed someone with experience. I stared at Cal; he looked at me for a second then looked away. I was sure he'd guessed what I was thinking but he just didn't want to know. He probably thought that he had to give Kris a bowl, but he should have brought her on earlier – anyone could see that.

Although he was captain I was surprised that he hadn't once turned to me for my advice. Marty appeared to agree with me. "I think Cal's losing his grip," he murmured as we crossed at the end of the sixteenth over. "They'll score 150 if he doesn't watch out."

I shrugged. "He's the captain."

"Yes, worse luck," moaned Marty.

Kris was very nervous. She missed her run up on the first attempt and ran straight through without releasing the ball. Then she bowled a half-volley which was cracked away for three through the covers. Cal went over and had a quiet word with her and so did Erica. With her second ball she found the spot. Three balls in a row went past the outside edge of the bat.

"That's the ball, Kris," said Erica encouragingly. "Keep it there." She did and would have had a wicket if Frankie hadn't fumbled a low chance to his left. Instead it ran away to third-man for a single. The final ball was a yorker on middle stump which the batsman only just dug out. Four runs off the over; this time Cal had been right I had to admit.

I was walking back to my fielding position at mid-off when he threw me the ball. "Last two overs at this end, Hooker," he said. "And keep it straight."

"But I thought Tylan was . . ."

"The trouble with you is that you can't count," said Cal. "I wanted you to bowl the last two, so I had to give Tylan one to make it up on overs. Just make sure you bowl better than that last lot of rubbish." He winked and slapped me on the back.

My plan was to bowl just short of a length on middle stump and throw in two yorkers an over and a slower one to keep the batters guessing. I pitched the first two a little too short and I was lucky they only cost me a run apiece. Then I bowled the slow one and it was hit straight in the air to Marty who put down a relatively easy catch. He was furious with himself and couldn't even look at me.

My first yorker didn't quite come off – it was more of a low full-toss and again it was worked away for a single. But with the last ball of the over I got it dead right. The ball swung late into the right-hander, went through the gate and flattened his off-stump. 89 for five.

Kris's last over was dead on target but the batsmen played their luck. A couple of edges, a bye and a dodgy run-out decision – and by the end of the over Cherrystanton had scratched another six runs.

I began my last six balls determined not to let them get the five runs they needed for their 100. My first delivery was the yorker again and it was squirted down to long-leg. The striker took on Azzie's throw for the second run . . . and lost. 96 for six.

I bowled another yorker at the incoming batsman and it just grazed past his off-stump. The next was the slow leg-break which he lobbed in the air just short of Clive. The Cherrystanton orders were obviously "swing at everything". A lucky flat-bat heave connected and the ball looped back over my head for two runs.

They were on 99. As I walked to my mark to bowl the last ball of the innings I thought, what is it to be? A yorker? The slow ball? Down the leg side? I went for a quick, straight delivery just short of a length. The batter played a horrible cow shot and got a top edge. The ball rose high in the direction of the covers between Mack and Erica. Mack called for it and ran. He wasn't going to make it. Or was he? He sprinted ten yards to his right and took off. As the ball dropped he met it in mid-air and held on with both hands. What a catch. It made us all feel we'd finished the innings on a high.

Mack keeps his eyes on the ball all the time. Look at the position of his hands as he takes the catch. What makes Mack such a good fielder is that he expects a catch from every ball. Because he's moving in as the ball is bowled, he's able to take up catching positions quickly and turn half chances into wickets.

"That's ten more runs than I wanted them to get," said Cal to me as we walked off. "It's my fault; my bowling was a bit loose and I shouldn't have brought Tylan back."

I smiled. "I shouldn't worry. I think you'll make a captain . . . one day. Anyway, we've knocked a hundred before – and we'll do it again today."

"Best get your pads on then, you're opening," said Cal.

HOME TEAM	CHERRYSTANTON	V	GLORY GARDENS	AWAY TEAM	AT EDGBASTON	DATE SEPTEMBER 12

INNINGS OF CHERRYSTANTON........ TOSS WON BY CHERRY WEATHER SUNNY.

BATSMAN	RUNS SCORED	HOW OUT	BOWLER	SCORE
1 A. BLACKMORE	2 >>	RUN	OUT	2
2 S. PITMAN	1.1.1.1.4.1.1.2.1.2.1.2.1.1 >>	ct McCURDY	DAVIES	20
3 J. PIKE	4.2.2.2.4.2.2.1.2.1.2.2.2.2 >>	RUN	OUT	30
4 S. MONK	>>	c & b	SEBASTIEN	0
5 B. POMFRETT	2.1.4.1.4.1.2.1.1.1 >>	bowled	KNIGHT	18
6 E. DIBDIN	2.1.3.1.1.1.1 >>	RUN	OUT	10
7 C. ORFE	2.1.2 >>	ct McCURDY	KNIGHT	5
8 B. MEANEY	1	NOT	OUT	1
9 P. PRYKKE				
10 P. ORFE				
11 F. DADE				

FALL OF WICKETS											BYES	3.2.1.1 ...		7	TOTAL EXTRAS	13
	1	2	3	4	5	6	7	8	9	10	L BYES	1.1.1		3	TOTAL FOR	99
SCORE	2	54	54	69	89	96	99				WIDES	1.1.1		3		
BAT NO	1	3	4	2	5	6	7				NO BALLS				WKTS	7

SCORE AT A GLANCE

BOWLER	BOWLING ANALYSIS · NO BALL - WIDE													OVS	MDS	RUNS	WKT
	1	2	3	4	5	6	7	8	9	10	11	12	13				
1 M. LEAR	...	.1.	...	M	X									4	1	7	0
2 H. KNIGHT	...	.12	11.	1.1										4	0	20	2
3 T. VELLACOTT	+..1	1.		14..	X									2.2	0	15	0
4 C. SEBASTIEN	14..	.12	2.	.21	X									3.4	0	23	1
5 E. DAVIES	..2	..2	.1.	1.1	X									4	0	15	1
6 K. JOHANSEN	3..	12.												2	0	9	0
7																	
8																	
9																	

Chapter Sixteen

"What's the big idea?" Clive asked Cal, seeing me putting on my pads.

"Simple," said Cal. "Hooker's our pinch hitter. I want to make sure we're up with the rate from the start."

"Why can't you be our what'd you call it?" Tylan asked Cal.

"Pinch hitter. It's the batter who smashes the bowling all over the ground at the start of an innings," said Matthew.

"I thought that was your job, Matt," said Frankie with a chuckle.

"I'm going six or seven in case there's a run chase at the end," said Cal.

This was his provisional batting order:

Matthew Rose
Hooker Knight
Azzie Nazar
Erica Davies
Clive da Costa
Cal Sebastien
Mack McCurdy
Kris Johansen
Frankie Allen
Tylan Vellacott
Marty Lear

Matthew took first strike and I watched the Cherrystanton

opening bowler run in. I was expecting something explosive and I wasn't wrong. Matthew did well to glove down a fast spitting ball bang on target. The next delivery took an outside edge and just beat slip diving full length. We ran a single. I think Matt was glad to get down to the other end.

I took a deep breath as the bowler ran in again. His speed surprised me and I was late in my stroke. The ball thudded into my pads and ran down the leg side. There was an enormous appeal. I knew it was close but Matthew called a single and I ran the leg-bye watching the umpire all the time. To my relief the finger stayed down. "Just down the leg side," he explained to the disbelieving bowler.

He wasn't just quick, he was swinging the ball, too. He beat the outside of Matthew's bat twice in a row and it was a bit of a miracle that we both survived the first over. The bowler certainly thought so; he gave me a big stare as if to say, what are you still doing here?

"Just dig in," I said to Matthew. "I'll try and knock them off their length."

"It would be easier if I could see them," said Matthew only half jokingly. "I hope the other bowler won't be as quick."

He wasn't – but he wasn't much slower and he too got a lot of bounce. Matthew edged another single and then I went after one well outside off-stump and top-edged over slip for four. It wasn't pretty but it was runs and we needed them badly.

Matthew continued to survive and not much else. He plays with virtually no back lift and he has a habit of pulling his bat inside the line of the ball at the last minute; so it looks as if he's playing and missing when he's not. But he wasn't going to score many runs; that was my job.

At last I got a ball of driveable length and played a nice shot into the covers off the middle of the bat – it made me feel a lot better. After four overs we had collected 12 runs but it wasn't enough. I knew the time had come when I had to start taking more risks to push the score along.

With Matthew at the other end, one of my biggest problems

was getting the strike. Matthew's never been the best picker of a short single. I called him through for a risky leg-bye and faced up to the demon fast bowler again. He bowled me a bouncer and I hooked. "Hooker, Hooker," the chant went up from the Glory Gardens players in the stand and the ball bounced once and over the boundary into the crowd. The large woman who had been in the midst of the Thimbledown "riot" was talking to someone behind her and the ball struck her on the back of her head – you could hear the crack from the middle. She jumped up and then slumped back in her seat again with a shrill cry.

I knew the next ball would be a yorker or another bouncer. It was the yorker and I dug it out just in time.

Playing a fast yorker calls for good reactions and technique. The first thing is to spot it. The ball is going to pitch near your batting crease and the temptation is to drive and play over the top of it. Instead you should jab your bat down on it like this.

Matthew was caught behind off the first ball of the next over and Azzie came out to join me. We were 18 for one.

Immediately the bowling looked different. Azzie's a class act. He has so much time and you hardly ever see him having to hurry. The lateness with which he plays his shots often frightens fast bowlers out of line. The second ball he received looked a goodish delivery until he wristed it off the top of the bounce with silky timing. We ran three.

I faced up to the last over from the demon of Cherrystanton. I wasn't quite sure, now Azzie was at the wicket, whether I should continue in my pinch-hitting job or just leave it to Az. It was probably that indecision which undid me. I got another short one and went to hook. It was on me faster than I expected and I pulled out of the shot. But as the ball passed over my shoulder I lost my balance and fell backwards. I knew in an instant that I was about to fall on the stumps so I tried to leap over them. I thought I was over . . . but no – one bail caught against my pad and, out of the corner of my eye I saw it falling to the ground. I was out - hit wicket.

I felt a bit silly as well as angry about the way I'd got out. I knew Frankie would say something daft when I got back.

"Cal thinks you were doing a cossack dance," he said with a smirk. "But I say it was Thai boxing. Which of us is right?" he said. I pretended not to hear and looked at Jo's score card. I'd made 13 out of the 22 runs we'd scored, but it was miles short of the innings Cal was expecting from me.

"Hitting that big woman must have broken your concentration," said Frankie.

"Yeah, probably cost me my fifty," I said.

"But it was worth it," said Tylan. "They had to carry her off."

Four balls later things went from bad to worse – Erica got an almost unplayable delivery which went straight through her and hit the top of the off-stump. Next ball Clive nearly followed her when he edged in the air between the keeper and slip; neither of them got a hand on it and it went behind for a single. That was the end of the demon, but his final over had practically settled the match. His figures were 4 overs, 10 runs, two wickets.

But Glory Gardens weren't finished yet. As long as Clive and Azzie were out there we had a chance. One, if not both of them, simply had to get a big score, mind – or we were definitely out of it.

Cherrystanton's two new bowlers were an interesting combination: a left-arm seamer and a left-arm wrist spinner. They were both fairly useful. The spinner had a very strange action – I think he bowled off the wrong foot. But he could certainly spin the ball – Clive told me afterwards he was turning it both ways.

A spinner can be a real problem when you're chasing a big total. You know you've got to get after him and the temptation is to try and hit the ball out of the ground. Half the time the result is that you spoon an easy catch or miss completely and get bowled.

Clive and Azzie were going along steadily when Clive suddenly had a rush of blood and darted down the pitch. The ball turned past his bat and he was stranded. It was a simple stumping chance for the keeper and to rub it in he did a "Frankie" and removed the bails with a great sweep of his arm, scattering the stumps everywhere. Then he threw the ball up in triumph and ran to congratulate the bowler.

We groaned. "That's torn it," said Cal; he slapped Mack on the shoulder. Mack had just been promoted to No. 6 ahead of Cal. "Tell Azzie I want him to bat out the innings. Your job's to hit anything loose out of the county. And best of luck."

With exactly half the overs gone we'd scored 36 for four. "That means we need 6.4 an over. It's not impossible," said Jo, putting a brave face on it.

Marty sighed. "Anything over six an over's going to be a nightmare against this standard of bowling. Particularly if we keep losing wickets."

"At least Azzie's still there," said Jacky.

Mack clouted his first ball for two past cover point and then pulled the next for four.

"I hope I haven't overdone the instructions," said Cal. "I didn't want him to bat like a windmill." Mack swung away at the next two deliveries and missed them both completely.

It was now Azzie's chance to show us how to handle the spinner. A delicate late-cut brought him two; then he glanced fine on the leg side and, when the bowler pitched up a bit too far on middle stump, he straight drove him majestically for four to bring up Glory Gardens' 50.

"The little master's starting to burn," said Tylan.

"If he stays, we win," said Jacky cheering a cheeky single as Azzie placed the ball between two of the in-fielders. In between bursts of Azzie's brilliance, Mack kept flailing away but he missed more than he hit and he was using up valuable balls that Azzie could have scored off.

"I wish he'd rotate the strike a bit more and let Azzie get at them," said Cal desperately looking at the score-board.

Finally Mack had one wild swing too many at the spinner and lost his leg stump. He may have got an inside edge but it was such a horrible shot he deserved to be out. At 56 for five, Cal went out to face his moment of truth.

"6.1 overs remaining; 44 to win at 7.14 runs an over," shouted Jo after him.

"Wind north-west force 3; visibility good," added Frankie for good measure.

Cal smiled. "Over and out. Wish me luck."

Jeremy Pike took over at the pavilion end. He was only medium pace, bowling little seamers, but he must have been moving the ball a bit because he went straight through Azzie with his second delivery and that's not easy when Az is in this form.

With the field out Cal and Azzie started pushing singles off every ball. They are both quick between the wickets and their tactics began to put pressure on the Cherrystanton fielders. But we couldn't win the game with singles; we needed a couple of boundaries badly and there hadn't been one for nearly five overs. With three overs left the run rate had now soared to 9.5

Jo's scoring-rate chart tells the story

	1	2	3	4	5	6	7	8	9	10	11	12	13	14	15	16	17	18	19	20
Cherrystanton	2	7	10	19	24	28	30	36	40	47	52	56	60	67	71	81	85	89	95	99
Glory Gardens	2	7	10	12	18	22	23	27	32	36	43	52	55	57	61	67	71			

an over.

"We'll never do it now," said Marty. "No chance."

"A quid says we will," said Frankie. "Especially if I get in."
He swung his bat wildly over his shoulder and nearly removed
Ohbert's head. Ohbert, of course, didn't notice.

A brilliant cover drive from Azzie almost went for four but a
great chase and dive limited it to three. Their fielding was
breathtaking. Apart from a couple of half-chances that went
down they didn't miss a thing.

Azzie changed tactics and began to play the gaps in the field –

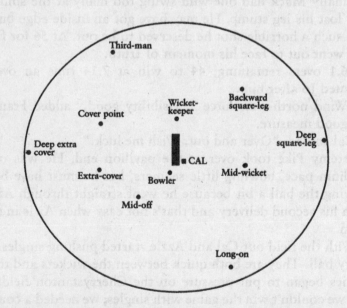

*Azzie looks for the gaps in the field – running the ball down to third-
man and long-on and then hitting over mid-off and extra-cover.*

hitting over the in-fielders and running the ball down to the boundary and taking two.

But he had to take chances to score off every ball. There were a lot of close calls and finally Azzie's luck ran out. His cover drive went straight to their best fielder who picked up on the run and threw at the bowler's stumps. Azzie dived full length but he was well out. He'd scored 32 and single-handedly just about kept us in the game.

"It's all up to Cal now," I said.

His new partner was Kris and she called for a single off the last ball of the over and, unfortunately, kept the strike. We now needed 20 from two overs.

Kris went down the pitch to Jeremy and blocked; Cal raced through for the single. Two more singles brought Cal back on strike. The fourth ball was short and Cal leaned back and cleared cover with a clean swing of the bat. The boundary fielder had no chance. A no ball and another single and we'd taken nine off the over. One to go.

The crowd was really buzzing now. Frankie and Tylan were both padded up. Frankie was taking bets on him scoring the winning runs. Marty was sitting with his head in his hands and Azzie was trying to shout instructions to Cal and Kris but no-one could hear him over the din.

There was a delay in the play. The Cherrystanton players were all standing in a circle arguing about something.

"I think they're looking for a new bowler," said Jo. "They're all bowled out except Jeremy Pike and he's on at the other end."

"Looks like a slip-up, Jeremy. Tut, tut," said Frankie.

It could be our chance, I thought, even if it was only a slim one. A fresh bowler could take a ball or two to find his length .. . and then, who knows?

Eventually Cherrystanton were ready. Their new bowler ran in off about eight paces and drifted one down the leg side. Cal clipped it just over square-leg's groping fingers for two.

There was a little conference in the middle between Kris and Cal before he faced the next ball. It was full length and Cal went for the big one but missed completely. Kris was backing up miles down the pitch and the keeper spotted her. In a flash he had his gloves off and threw to the bowler's end. Kris grounded her bat seconds after the ball hit the stumps. Another direct throw on target had cost us a wicket.

Frankie swaggered out to the middle, bat across his shoulders, arms hooked round it. If he was nervous he certainly wasn't showing it. Four balls left and we still needed 9 runs. Cal had a word with Frankie and settled to face the bowling. Again the ball went down the leg side and the keeper fumbled. Frankie was through for the bye before the umpire called "wide" – a pity because it took Cal off strike.

Frankie didn't bother with a guard; he stood with his bat raised high and waited. The bowler dropped the ball in just the right spot for him – through came the big swing and, one, two bounces and there was the four we needed. The cheers erupted and Frankie received them with a swing of his bat and a wide smile.

Four to win and no secret how Frankie planned to do it. His haymaking swing would have finished it with a six if he had connected. But he didn't. The ball went straight through and clattered his stumps. The groan was almost as loud as the cheer for the last shot.

Tylan set off for the middle immediately. He didn't wait for us to give him his instructions. His nose was glowing brightly in the evening light but his face was white and tense. A slap on the back from Frankie and a quiet word from Cal and he took guard. Four to win and two balls remaining.

"He 'nose' what he's got to do," said Frankie rejoining us in the pavilion stand. We ignored him.

Tylan's not a hopeless bat but his run scoring record isn't brilliant. The main thing was for him to hit the ball somewhere and run. He got it high on the bat and it lobbed away in the air but exactly between two fielders. It was an easy single but two was out of the question.

You could almost see the relief in Ty's face to have escaped from the strike.

"Come on, Cal, three to win. Make it a six," shrieked Frankie. There was a long delay again as the Cherrystanton fielders all moved out to the boundary. If Cal didn't hit a six it was hard to see where he was going to score the runs.

"Maybe he should settle for two and a tie," said Marty.

Frankie threw a cricket ball at him and just missed his head. "We're not playing safe. It's death or glory for Glory Gardens."

I favoured the hit over extra-cover for four. Azzie said the straight drive back over the bowler's head was the answer. The bowler began his last approach. A hush fell across the ground. The ball was on a length and Cal went for the sweep shot. He got a fair amount of bat on it and it went fast and fine to the keeper's left. Cal sprinted down the track.

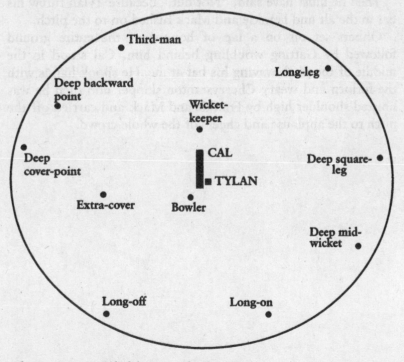

Cherrystanton fielding in the last over

Both the keeper and long-leg were after the ball. Cal and Tylan turned simultaneously for the second.

"Three it," shouted Frankie.

"No, two," cried Marty.

The long-leg fielder won the chase and picked up just inside the boundary. It was Tylan's call for the third run but he didn't utter a word. Down went his head and he ran. The throw came in first bounce but a little wide of the stumps.

"Dive. Dive," shouted Frankie.

Tylan dived. He took off about three yards short of the crease and his outstretched bat slid across the line. The bails flew in the air.

"In!" screamed Frankie. And we all looked at the square-leg umpire. His hand came out of his pocket and my heart stopped.

Then he must have said, "Not out," because Tylan threw his bat in the air and Frankie and Mack rushed on to the pitch.

Ohbert set off on a lap of honour of the entire ground followed by Gatting wobbling behind him. Cal stood in the middle of the pitch waving his bat at me. He shook hands with the forlorn and weary Cherrystanton skipper and then he was hoisted shoulder high by Frankie and Mack and carried off the pitch to the applause and cheers of the whole crowd.

| HOME TEAM CHERRY STANTON | V | GLORY GARDENS | AWAY TEAM | AT EDGBASTON DATE SEPTEMBER 10 |

INNINGS OF GLORY GARDENS   TOSS WON BY CHERRY   WEATHER SUNNY

BATSMAN	RUNS SCORED	HOW OUT	BOWLER	SCORE
1 M.ROSE	1·1·1·1 >> . — .. . . . —	ct DIBDIN	ORFE	4
2 H.KNIGHT	4·2·1·1·4·1 >> . .	hit wkt	MEANEY	13
3 A.NAZAR	3·1·1·2·1·1·2·2·4·1·1·1·1·1·1·1·1 >> 3·2·2	RUN	OUT	32
4 E.DAVIES	>> — . — — ..	bowled	MEANEY	0
5 C.DA.COSTA	1·2·1·2·1·1 >> — . —	st DIBDIN	PRYKKE	8
6 T.McCURDY	2·4·2 >> — . . — ..	bowled	PRYKKE	8
7 C.SEBASTIEN	1·1·1·2·1·1·1·1·1·4·1·2·3 _ ..	NOT	OUT	20
8 K.JOHANSEN	1·1 >> . — — . — .	RUN	OUT	2
9 F.ALLEN	4 >> . — — — . — ..	bowled	POMFRETT	4
10 T.VELLACOTT	1· . — . . .	NOT	OUT	1
11 M.LEAR	. . — .			

FALL OF WICKETS

	1	2	3	4	5	6	7	8	9	10
SCORE	18	22	22	36	56	79	91	96		
BAT NO	1	2	4	5	6	3	8	9		

BYES	— . . — ..	8 TOTAL EXTRAS
L BYES	1·1·1·1·1	5 TOTAL 100
WIDES	1	1 FOR
NO BALLS	1·1	2 8 WKTS

SCORE AT A GLANCE

BOWLER	BOWLING ANALYSIS · NO BALL · WIDE													OVS	MDS	RUNS	WKT
	1	2	3	4	5	6	7	8	9	10	11	12	13				
1 B.MEANEY	:·:	··1 ·2·	1·· ·4·	W··· ·W1	X									4	0	10	2
2 P.ORFE	··· 14·	1·· 1·1	W·3 ··	2·· ·11	X									4	0	15	1
3 F.DADE	·O·· 2·1	·12 4···	·1· 2··	X	2·2 2·1									4	0	24	0
4 P.PRYKKE	12· 1·W	2·2 6·1	·1· ·W·	121 ·11										4	0	20	2
5 J.PIKE	··1 111	·1· 1··	111 4O1·											3	0	15	0
6 B.POMFRETT	2··4 W13													1	0	11	1
7																	
8																	
9																	

Chapter Seventeen

Two hours later we were on the bus home.

"I still can't believe it," said Cal. "It must be a dream. Pinch me someone." Frankie did – very hard. "Okay, I believe it," winced Cal.

"It's real all right. Here's the trophy to prove it," said Azzie holding up the big silver plate. "It says 'Under 13 Champion of Champions'. And there's the space where they'll put Glory Gardens C.C."

"It's a pity Cal dropped it when Nick Knight did the presentation," said Tylan. "See, it's got a dent in it."

"I can't wait to see it hanging up in the Priory pavilion," said Marty. "I always had a feeling we were going to win it." He ducked behind his seat to avoid the barrage of missiles.

Frankie celebrated the occasion with another of his awful calypsos.

> *Glory Gardens came to Edgbaston*
> *Their chances were a hundred to one*
> *But in the final they scored a ton*
> *And beat the favourites from Cherrystanton.*
>
> *But everybody remember that*
> *Their heads were down they were feeling flat*
> *Till along came Ohbert with a well-timed kick*
> *And Jeremy left looking very sick.*

There were lots more verses, several of them about Frankie

himself, but I've forgotten them. It was a lively journey home with everyone remembering something different about the day at Edgbaston. My golden moment was my partnership with Ohbert against Thimbledown. But I'd never forget Marty's bowling in the same game or Azzie's knock in the final.

We'd all received individual medals, including Jacky and Ohbert and most of us were still wearing them round our necks. Ohbert couldn't stop looking at his. He'd even switched his Walkman off so that he could concentrate on it properly.

We hadn't awarded a Player of the Match award for any of the games at Edgbaston; we'd been too busy to think about it. So now we voted on Player of the Day. When the votes were counted it was scored like this:

Ohbert	4
Erica	3
Hooker	2
Marty	1
Azzie	1
Cal	1
Gatting	1

It was a popular, if unexpected, choice and Ohbert was crowned with the Player of the Day cap. He sat there with his medal round his neck and the silver plate in his arms looking like the king of Glory Gardens.

"What's it like to be famous, Ohbert?" asked Frankie.

Ohbert looked at him blankly.

"Now everyone will want your autograph," said Tylan.

"Oh but . . . will they?" said Ohbert.

"You bet," said Mack.

"Oh but, I'd better practise it then," said Ohbert. And that's what he did all the way home.

BATTING AVERAGES

	INNS	N.O.	RUNS	S.R.	H.S.	AVERAGE
Erica	5	1	95	61	54*	23.75
Hooker	4	1	71	88	44*	23.67
Clive	5	0	108	95	59	21.60
Azzie	4	0	59	96	32	14.75
Cal	5	1	46	52	20*	11.50
Mack	5	1	33	54	22*	8.25
Frankie	5	0	38	112	12	7.60

*denotes 'not out'. Scoring rate (S.R.) is based on the average number of runs scored per 100 balls. H.S. = highest score. Minimum qualification: 30 runs.

Highest individual scores

Clive	59		v Saracens
Erica	54*	v Saracens	
Hooker	44*	v Thimbledown	

Highest partnerships:

Clive and Erica	59	v Saracens
Erica and Kris	41*	v Saracens
Clive and Mack	30	v Old Bodilians

Fastest 50 Clive	59	v Saracens

BOWLING AVERAGES

	OVERS	MAIDENS	RUNS	WICKETS	ECON	S.R.	AVE
Marty	16	1	58	8	3.6	12.0	7.3
Hooker	13	0	48	6	3.7	13.0	8.0
Tylan	14.2	0	59	5	4.1	17.2	11.8
Cal	22.4	1	90	5	4.0	27.2	18.0
Erica	26	5	63	3	2.4	52.0	21.0

Strike rate (S.R.) is the average number of balls bowled to take each wicket. Economy rate (Econ) is the average number of runs given away each over. Minimum qualification: 3 wickets.

Best bowling:

Marty 5 for 12 v Thimbledown
Tylan 3 for 21 v Saracens
Hooker 2 for 4 v Thimbledown

Best economy bowling

Erica 8 overs, 10 runs v Old Bodilians
Jacky 8 overs, 13 runs v Old Bodilians
Erica 6 overs, 8 runs v Saracens

Catches

	CAUGHT	DROPPED	TOTAL
Azzie	2	0	+2
Erica	2	0	+2
Mack	2	0	+2
Marty	2	1	+1
Cal	1	0	+1
Jacky	1	0	+1
Kris	1	0	+1
Tylan	2	2	0
Frankie	4	5	-1
Kipper	0	1	-1
Ohbert	0	3	-3

THE CRICKET PITCH

crease

At each end of the wicket the crease is marked out in white paint like this:

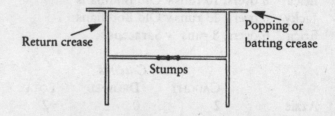

Return crease

Popping or batting crease

Stumps

The batsman is 'in his ground' when his bat or either foot are behind the batting or 'popping' crease. He can only be given out 'stumped' or 'run out' if he is outside the crease. The bowler must not put his front foot down beyond the popping crease when he bowls. And his back foot must be inside the return crease. If he breaks these rules the umpire will call a 'no ball'.

leg side/ off-side

The cricket pitch is divided down the middle. Everything on the side of the batsman's legs in called the 'leg side' or 'on side' and the other side is called the 'off-side'.

Remember, when a left-handed bat is batting, his legs are on the other side. So leg side and off-side switch round.

leg stump

Three stumps and two bails make up each wicket. The 'leg stump' is on the same side as the batsman's legs. Next to it is the 'middle stump' and then the 'off stump'.

off/on side	See **leg side**.
off-stump	See **leg stump**.
pitch	The 'pitch' is the area between the two wickets. It is 22 yards long from wicket to wicket (although it's usually 20 yards for Under 11s and 21 yards for Under 13s). The grass on the pitch is closely mown and rolled flat. Just to make things confusing, sometimes the whole ground is called a 'cricket pitch'.
square	The area in the centre of the ground where the strips are.
strip	Another name for the pitch. They are called strips because there are several pitches side by side on the square. A different one is used for each match.
track	Another name for the pitch or strip.
wicket	'Wicket' means two things, so it can sometimes confuse people. 1 The stumps and the bails at each end of the pitch. The batsman defends his wicket. 2 The pitch itself. So you can talk about a hard wicket or a turning wicket (if it's taking spin).

BATTING

attacking strokes	The attacking strokes in cricket all have names. There are forward strokes (played off the front foot) and backward strokes (played off the back foot).

139

The drawing shows where the different strokes are played around the wicket.

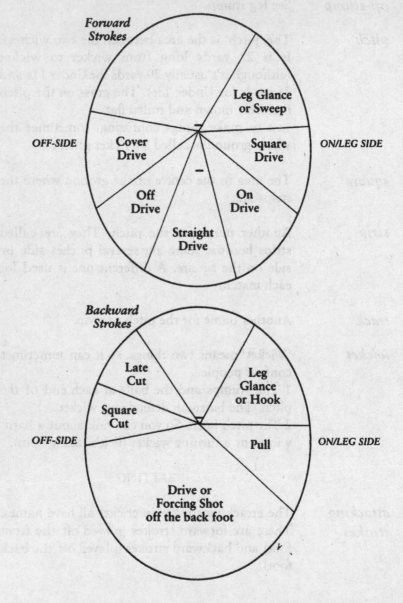

Forward Strokes

OFF-SIDE | ON/LEG SIDE

Leg Glance or Sweep

Cover Drive

Square Drive

Off Drive

On Drive

Straight Drive

Backward Strokes

OFF-SIDE | ON/LEG SIDE

Late Cut

Leg Glance or Hook

Square Cut

Pull

Drive or Forcing Shot off the back foot

backing up   As the bowler bowls, the non-striking batsman should start moving down the wicket to be ready to run a quick single. This is called 'backing up'.

bye   If the ball goes past the bat and the keeper misses it, the batsman can run a 'bye'. If it hits the batsman's pad or any part of his body (apart from his glove), the run is called a 'leg-bye'. Byes and leg-byes are put in the 'Extras' column in the score-book. They are not credited to the batsman or scored against the bowler's analysis.

This is how an umpire will signal a bye and leg-bye

Bye

Leg-bye

cart   To hit a ball a very long way.

centre   See **guard**.

chinese cut   If a batsman plays an attacking shot on the off side and gets an inside edge past his stumps, it is sometimes called a 'chinese cut'.

141

cow shot	When the batsman swings across the line of a delivery, aiming towards mid-wicket, it is often called a 'cow shot'.
defensive strokes	There are basically two defensive shots: the 'forward defensive', played off the front foot and the 'backward defensive' played off the back foot.
duck	When a batsman is out before scoring any runs it's called a 'duck'. If he's out first ball for nought it's a 'golden duck'.
flat-back	To hit the ball back down under the wicket with a horizontal rather than straight bat.
gate	If a batsman is bowled after the ball has passed between his bat and pads it is sometimes described as being bowled 'through the gate'.
guard	When you go in to bat the first thing you do is 'take your guard'. You hold your bat sideways in front of the stumps and ask the umpire to give you a guard. He'll show you which way to move the bat until it's in the right position. The usual guards are 'leg stump' (sometimes called 'one leg'); 'middle and leg' ('two leg') and 'centre' or 'middle'.

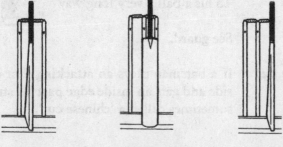

Centre   Middle and leg   Leg

hit wicket	If the batsman knocks off a bail with his bat or any part of his body when the ball is in play, he is out 'hit wicket'.
innings	This means a batsman's stay at the wicket. 'It was the best *innings* I'd seen Azzie play.' But it can also mean the batting score of the whole team. 'In their first *innings* England scored 360.'
knock	Another word for a batsman's innings.
lbw	Means leg before wicket. In fact a batsman can be given out lbw if the ball hits any part of his body and the umpire thinks it would have hit the stumps. There are two important extra things to remember about lbw: 1 If the ball pitches outside the leg stump and hits the batsman's pads it's not out - even if the ball would have hit the stumps. 2 If the ball pitches outside the off-stump and hits the pad outside the line, it's not out if the batsman is playing a shot. If he's not playing a shot he can still be given out.
leg-bye	See bye.
middle/ *middle & leg*	See **guard**.
out	There are six common ways of a batsman being given out in cricket: bowled, caught, lbw, hit wicket, run out and stumped. Then there are a few rare ones like handled the ball and hit the ball twice. When the fielding side thinks the batsman is out they must appeal (usually a shout of 'Owzthat').

143

If the umpire considers the batsman is out, he will signal 'out' like this:

play forward/back	You play forward by moving your front foot down the wicket towards the bowler as you play the ball. You play back by putting your weight on the back foot and leaning towards the stumps. You play forward to well-pitched-up bowling and back to short-pitched bowling.
rabbit	Poor or tail-end batsman.
run	A run is scored when the batsman hits the ball and runs the length of the pitch. If he fails to reach the popping crease before the ball is thrown in and the bails are taken off, he is 'run out'. Four runs are scored when the ball is hit across the boundary. Six runs are scored when it crosses the boundary without bouncing. This is how the umpire signals 'four':

This is how the umpire signals 'six'.

If the batsman does not put his bat down inside the popping crease at the end of a run before setting off on another run, the umpire will signal 'one short' like this.

A run is then deducted from the total by the scorer.

stance   The stance is the way a batsman stands and holds his bat when he is waiting to receive a delivery. There are many different types of stance. For instance, 'side on', with the shoulder pointing down the wicket; 'square on', with the body turned towards the bowler'; 'bat raised' and so on.

145

striker	The batsman who is receiving the bowling. The batsman at the other end is called the non-striker.
stumped	If you play and miss and the wicket-keeper knocks a bail off with the ball in his hands, you will be out 'stumped' if you are out of your crease.
ton	A century. One hundred runs scored by a batsman.

BOWLING

arm ball	A variation by the off-spinner (or left-arm spinner) which swings in the air in the opposite direction to the normal spin, ie away from the right-handed batsman in the case of the off-spinner.
beamer	See full toss.
block hole	A ball bowled at yorker length is said to pitch in the 'block hole' - ie the place where the batsman marks his guard and rests his bat on the ground when receiving.
bouncer	The bowler pitches the ball very short and bowls it hard into the ground to get extra bounce and surprise the batsman. The ball will often reach the batsman at shoulder height or above. But you have to be a fast bowler to bowl a good bouncer. A slow bouncer is often called a 'long hop' and is easy to pull or cut for four.

chinaman   A left-arm bowler who bowls with the normal leg-break action will deliver an off-break to the right-handed batsman. This is called a 'chinaman'.

dot ball   A ball from which the batsman does not score a run. It is called this because it goes down as a dot in the score-book.

flipper   A variation on the leg-break. It is bowled from beneath the wrist, squeezed out of the fingers, and it skids off the pitch and goes straight through. It shouldn't be attempted by young cricketers because it puts a lot of strain on the wrist and arm ligaments.

full toss   A ball which doesn't bounce before reaching the batsman is a full toss. Normally it's easy to score off a full toss, so it's considered a bad ball. A high full toss from a fast bowler is called a 'beamer'. It is very dangerous and should never be bowled deliberately.

googly   A 'googly' is an off-break bowled with a leg break action (see leg break) out of the back of the hand like this.

grubber	A ball which hardly bounces - it pitches and shoots through very low, usually after hitting a bump or crack in the pitch. Sometimes also called a shooter.
hat trick	Three wickets from three consecutive balls by one bowler. They don't have to be in the same over ie two wickets from the last two balls of one over and one from the first of the next
half-volley	See **length**
leg break/ off-break	The 'leg break' is a delivery from a spinner which turns from leg to off. An 'off-break' turns from off to leg. That's easy to remember when it's a right-hand bowler bowling to a right-hand batsman. But when a right-arm, off-break bowler bowls to a left-handed bat he is bowling leg-breaks. And a left-hander bowling with an off-break action bowls leg-breaks to a right-hander. It takes some working out- but the drawing helps.

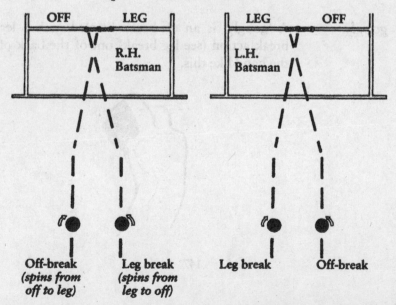

leg-cutter/ *off-cutter*	A ball which cuts away off the pitch from leg to off is a 'leg-cutter'. The 'off-cutter' goes from off to leg. Both these deliveries are bowled by fast or medium-paced bowlers. See **seam bowling**.
leggie	Slang for a leg-spin bowler.
length	You talk about the 'length' or 'pitch' of a ball bowled. A good length ball is one that makes the batsman unsure whether to play back or forward. A short-of-a-length ball pitches slightly closer to the bowler than a good length. A very short-pitched ball is called a 'long hop'. A 'half-volley' is an over-pitched ball which bounces just in front of the batsman and is easy to drive.
long hop	A ball which pitches very short. See **length**.
maiden over	If a bowler bowls an over without a single run being scored off the bat, it's called a 'maiden over'. It's still a maiden if there are byes or leg-byes but not if the bowler gives away a wide.
no ball	'No ball' can be called for many reasons. 1 The most common is when the bowler's front foot goes over the popping crease at the moment of delivery. It is also a no ball if he steps on or outside the return crease. See **crease**. 2 If the bowler throws the ball instead of bowling it. If the arm is straightened during the bowling action it is a throw. 3 If the bowler changes from bowling over the wicket to round the wicket (or vice versa) without telling the umpire.

149

4 If there are more than two fielders behind square on the leg side. (There are other fielding regulations with the limited overs game. For instance, the number of players who have to be within the circle.)

A batsman can't be out off a no ball, except run out. A penalty of one run (an experiment of two runs is being tried in county cricket) is added to the score and an extra ball must be bowled in the over. The umpire shouts 'no ball' and signals like this:

over the wicket   If a right-arm bowler delivers the ball from the right of the stumps (as seen by the batsman) ie with his bowling arm closest to the stumps, then he is bowling 'over the wicket'. If he bowls from the other side of the stumps he is bowling 'round the wicket'.

pace   The pace of the ball is the speed it is bowled at. A fast or pace bowler like Waqar Younis can bowl at speeds of up to 90 miles and hour. The different speeds of bowlers range from fast through medium to slow with in-between speeds like fast-medium and medium-fast (fast-medium is the faster).

pitch	See **length**.
reverse swing	Reverse swing occurs when the ball is old and one side of it has become roughed up. Under these conditions some fast bowlers will make the ball swing away from the roughed-up side of the ball. No-one really knows why it happens.
round the wicket	See **over the wicket**
seam	The seam is the sewn, raised ridge which runs round a cricket ball.
seam bowling	Bowling – usually medium to fast – where the ball cuts into or away from the batsman off the seam.
shooter	See **grubber**.
spell	A 'spell' of bowling is the number of overs bowled in succession by a bowler. So if a bowler bowls six overs before being replaced by another bowler, he has bowled a spell of six overs.
swing bowling	A cricket ball can be bowled to swing through the air. It has to be bowled in a particular way to achieve this and one side of the ball must be polished and shiny. Which is why you always see fast bowlers shining the ball. An 'in-swinger' swings into the batsman's legs from the off-side. An 'out-swinger' swings away towards the slips.
trundler	A steady, medium-pace bowler who is not particularly good.
turn	

turned a long way' or 'it spun a long way'.

wicket maiden	An over when no run is scored off the bat and the bowler takes one wicket or more.
wide	If the ball is bowled too far down the leg side or the off-side for the batsman to reach (usually the edge of the return crease is the line umpires look for) it is called a 'wide'. One run is added to the score and an extra ball is bowled in the over. In limited overs cricket wides are given for balls closer to the stumps - any ball bowled down the leg side risks being called a wide in this sort of 'one-day' cricket. This is how an umpire signals a wide.

yorker	A ball, usually a fast one - bowled to bounce precisely under the batsman's bat. The most dangerous yorker is fired in fast towards the batsman's legs to hit leg stump.

FIELDING

backing up	A fielder backs up a throw to the wicket-keeper or bowler by making sure it doesn't go for overthrows. So when a throw comes in to the keeper, a fielder is positioned behind him to cover him if he misses it. Not to be confused with a *batsman* backing up.

chance	A catchable ball. So to miss a chance is the same as to drop a catch.
close/deep	Fielders are either placed close to the wicket (near the batsman) or in the deep or 'out-field' (near the boundary).
cow corner	The area between the deep mid-wicket and long-on boundaries where a *cow shot* is hit to.
dolly	An easy catch.
hole-out	A slang expression for a batsman being caught. 'He holed out at mid-on.'
overthrow	If the ball is thrown to the keeper or the bowler's end and is misfielded allowing the batsmen to take extra runs, these are called 'overthrows'.
silly	A fielding position very close to the batsman and in front of the wicket eg silly mid-on.
sledging	Using abusive language and swearing at a batsman to put him off. A slang expression – first used in Australia.
square	Fielders 'square' of the wicket are on a line with the batsman on either side of the wicket. If they are fielding further back from this line, they are 'behind square' or 'backward of square'; if they are fielding in front of the line ie closer to the bowler, they are 'in front of square' or 'forward of square'.
standing up/ standing back	The wicket-keeper 'stands up' to the stumps for slow bowlers. This means he takes his position

immediately behind the stumps. For fast bowlers he stands well back – often several yards for very quick bowlers. He may either stand up or back for medium-pace bowlers.

GENERAL WORDS

colts County Colts teams are selected from the best young cricketers in the county at all ages from Under 11 to Under 17. Junior league cricket is usually run by the County Colts Association.

under 11s/ You qualify for an Under 11 team if you are 11
12s etc or under on September 1st prior to the cricket season. So if you're 12 but you were 11 on September 1st last year, you can play for the Under 11s.

FIELDING POSITIONS

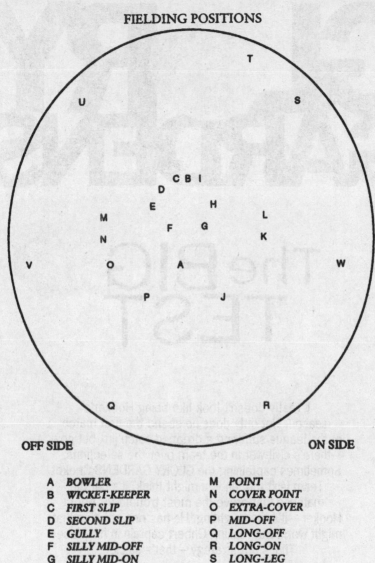

OFF SIDE   **ON SIDE**

A	*BOWLER*	M	*POINT*
B	*WICKET-KEEPER*	N	*COVER POINT*
C	*FIRST SLIP*	O	*EXTRA-COVER*
D	*SECOND SLIP*	P	*MID-OFF*
E	*GULLY*	Q	*LONG-OFF*
F	*SILLY MID-OFF*	R	*LONG-ON*
G	*SILLY MID-ON*	S	*LONG-LEG*
H	*BACKWARD SHORT LEG*	T	*DEEP FINE-LEG*
I	*LEG SLIP*	U	*THIRD-MAN*
J	*MID-ON*	V	*DEEP EXTRA COVER*
K	*MID-WICKET*	W	*DEEP MID-WICKET*
L	*SQUARE-LEG*		

GLORY GARDENS

The BIG TEST

It really doesn't look like being Hooker's season. Not only does he spend the first match of the league suffering a dropped-catch jinx but now there's civil war in the team over the selections. Sometimes captaining the GLORY GARDENS Cricket Team isn't the fun you might think. It's not the matches that prove the most trouble for poor Hooker – it's the infighting. He has one solution that might work. But making Ohbert captain in his place? That's not strategy – that's suicide.

ISBN 0-09-9-946131-5   **RED FOX**   £ 4.99

GLORY GARDENS

World Cup FEVER

• • • • • • • • • • • • • • •

GLORY GARDENS C.C. can't resist a challenge
and this time they're going for gold in a World Cup
competition! With teams from Barbados and South Africa
visiting the area at the same time, it's a brilliant
opportunity for the club to make its mark worldwide.
It's not long before the thrills and spills of cricket spark
off sporting drama, temper tantrums and practical jokes.
So, as Australia do battle with the West Indies and
South Africa face India, can Glory Gardens rise above
the squabbling and bring glory for England...?

• • • • • • • • • • • • • • •

ISBN 0-09-946141-2   **RED FOX**   £ 4.99

GLORY GARDENS

Down the WICKET

• • • • • • • • • • • •

On returning from their West Indies tour, the players in
GLORY GARDENS C. C. are devastated to learn that
their ground has been sold. Although the senior club disbands,
the team are determined to find a new home and, led by Jo,
they vote to play the season's league games on the recreation
ground where the club first began. But the pitch is dreadful,
the changing rooms a disgrace and, with their best batsmen
threatening to leave, some drastic action is called for...

• • • • • • • • • • • • • • • •

ISBN 0-09-940903-8   **RED FOX**   £ 4.99